"So the best part of giving people pleasure?"

Daniel's grin made Angela catch her breath. His blue eyes had caught the late evening light. His white teeth were surrounded by golden, smoothly shaved skin that looked as if it smelled and tasted wonderful. Angela felt as if her body had stopped functioning. Certainly her brain had.

Daniel knelt at her feet; his fingers landed softly on her bare knee, shooting Angela through with arousal as if he'd touched her...somewhere else.

"I think you could give me a lot of pleasure." His voice was low and slightly husky, his eyes didn't leave hers, so blue and so serious, humor dancing at their edges.

Angela's cue. Her hands landed on the firm planes of Daniel's pecs, her mouth lifted toward his. "I think I'd like to."

"But..."

"No." She put her finger to his lips, heart thudding. "We're here, Daniel, you and I. We're alive and we're together. This is supposed to happen. For both of us."

"You're okay with this?" Just to be sure.

"Yes." He murmured the word without hesitation; his hand cupped the back of her neck and he bent to her mouth, his lips sure and sweet.

Dear Reader,

When I visited a friend in Seattle a few summers
ago, I knew I had to set a book there. After the idea
came to me for a miniseries about friends whose
businesses represent the five senses, I realized I
could set three books there! It's a great town, clean,
green and close to one of my favorite things in the
world: the ocean.

Of course the five friends who own the Come to
Your Senses building not only explore Seattle's
great food, coffee and hot spots, they also find
love. In this first book, *Just One Kiss,* expert baker
Angela struggles with wonderful and sometimes
overwhelming feelings for the unexpectedly sexy
Daniel, who, finally throwing off past grief, is ready
to taste everything she has to offer.

It's very exciting starting a new series. I hope you
enjoy all the books in Friends with Benefits!

Cheers,

Isabel Sharpe

www.IsabelSharpe.com

Isabel Sharpe

JUST ONE KISS

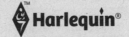

TORONTO NEW YORK LONDON
AMSTERDAM PARIS SYDNEY HAMBURG
STOCKHOLM ATHENS TOKYO MILAN MADRID
PRAGUE WARSAW BUDAPEST AUCKLAND

Recycling programs
for this product may
not exist in your area.

ISBN-13: 978-0-373-79680-9

JUST ONE KISS

Copyright © 2012 by Muna Shehadi Sill

ABOUT THE AUTHOR

Isabel Sharpe was not born pen in hand like so many of her fellow writers. After she quit work to stay home with her firstborn son and nearly went out of her mind, she started writing. After more than twenty novels for Harlequin—along with another son—Isabel is more than happy with her choice these days. She loves hearing from readers. Write to her at www.IsabelSharpe.com.

Books by Isabel Sharpe

HARLEQUIN BLAZE

*Men to Do
†Do Not Disturb
**The Wrong Bed
††The Martini Dares
§Forbidden Fantasies
§§The Wrong Bed: Again & Again
~Checking E-Males

To Mark, who, among many other
wonderful qualities, puts out a good bake.

"YOU ARE WELCOME." Angela Loukas handed the plump waxed bag across her sparkling glass counter to her favorite customer, Marjorie. The seventy-something woman came daily to Angela's bakery, A Taste for All Pleasures, between 5:00 and 6:00 p.m. for her next-day's breakfast—today a cinnamon-pecan roll. Given that Marjorie weighed about a hundred pounds, Angela worried the bakery items were all she was eating. "Would you like a black-pepper fruit tart for dessert tonight?"

"Oh…" Marjorie glanced doubtfully at the tiny tarts—raspberries, blueberries, kiwi slices and mandarin sections glistening with currant jelly glaze and speckled with crushed black peppercorns.

"On the house," Angela said impulsively. "For a loyal customer."

"Oh, well. I can't say no to that." She reached to accept the tart, fragile hand bones extending from her flawlessly tailored coral linen suit. "I'll eat it right away. It looks too good to wait."

"I hope you enjoy it."

Marjorie took a bite and chewed carefully. "Hmm. Yes.

Very nice. But your muffins are exquisite. And those cinnamon rolls…my goodness. As if God had smiled on them."

Angela kept her expression warm, but her heart sank. God hadn't smiled on the tarts? Maybe she needed to revise the recipe yet again. "Thank you, that's very sweet."

"You're welcome. I'll see you tomorrow, Angela, dear."

"See you then." Angela waved the tiny woman out of the shop, still pondering the reaction. She'd added the new section of European pastries to her year-old bakery in the last few months. So far, in spite of low prices and occasional giveaways, and in spite of Seattle's relatively sophisticated population, her customers still seemed to prefer the standard cookies, muffins, cupcakes, simple breads and other familiar baked goods she'd started with while she built confidence.

Her dream was to turn A Taste for All Pleasures into a European-style bakery known city-wide for its selection, quality and aesthetics.

Not there yet, but she wasn't giving up.

Her door chime began a phrase from one of Angela's favorite songs, Green Day's "Wake Me Up When September Ends." Seth Blackstone, whose music studio was upstairs in the building, had rigged the notifier to play her favorites when customers came in.

Angela's welcoming smile got wider when she saw Bonnie Fortuna, gifted florist and owner of Bonnie Blooms, the shop opposite hers in the building she and four other entrepreneurial friends who'd graduated from Washington University together had bought a year before. Four businesses were arranged on the first floor, with individual apartments and Seth's studio/apartment combination on the upper.

"Hey, Bonnie. How's things today?"

"All good." Bonnie stood in the center of the bakery, wearing her trademark hodgepodge of styles and colors, proffering a vase of burgundy and pink alstroemeria. "Thought you'd like these. Maybe over by the coffee?"

"Ooh, those would look great, thanks." She watched Bonnie rotate the black-and-silver vase on the high counter until the arrangement sat just right against her faintly rose-colored walls. "Would you by any chance be hoping to trade for a cookie?"

"A cookie. Well…" Bonnie gave the flowers one last look and nodded her satisfaction. "I could find uses for a cookie. Especially if it happens to be walnut-chocolate-chunk."

"It does." Angela handed one over. "What's new?"

"Wait, let me concentrate." Bonnie bit into her cookie and closed her green eyes rapturously, a smile curving her bright red lips. "*Ohhh,* these are so amazing. You are Seattle's cookie queen."

"Thanks." Angela leaned her elbows on the counter next to the register. Cookies. Yeah. Ordinary, everyday recipes she could make in her sleep. "So what's going on? Did that guy you met dancing ever ask you out?"

"Oh, him. Yeah, sort of." Bonnie made a face.

"And…?"

Bonnie studied her alternating scarlet and black fingernails a little too carefully. "I wasn't really feeling it."

"Why not? You don't have to marry him, just go out."

"Hmm "

"Geez, Bonnie. You can't sit around the rest of your life wait—" She stopped herself from blurting out her suspicion that Bonnie was still waiting five years later for their resident musician, Seth, whom she dated junior year until he freaked out over how serious the relationship was getting. Bonnie hadn't come close to being serious about anyone else since. "You can't avoid men forever."

"I've dated plenty. What about *you?* You're not exactly pouncing on single guys, either."

"I'm not…ready." Angela winced at how lame the excuse sounded. She'd been divorced for three years, after nine months of a dream-come-true marriage that turned nightmare when Tom was unfaithful with the exact type of woman his parents had wanted him to marry in the first place. Annabel, aka The Princess, was tall, WASPy and aristocratic, with strawberry-blond hair, flawless skin and an inheritance the size of her chilly conceit. While there sat half-Greek wallflower Angela Loukas—not tall, not blond, not rich, not chic, and worst of all, not perfect.

"Tom was a dork." Bonnie glanced longingly at the cookies, separated from her by a cold, uncaring pane of glass. "You can do sooo much better than him."

"Maybe. If I wanted to try." She reached down and pulled out another walnut-chocolate-chunk. "It's tough to recover from that much fun."

"Oh, come on. You're telling me if the perfect man walked through that door tomorrow and asked you out you'd turn him down?"

"Ha!" Angela handed the cookie over. "First of all, I matured out of the perfect-man fantasy when Tom came home late with hickeys all over him."

"Ew." Bonnie grimace melted into bliss when she started in on the second cookie.

"I was so naive I thought there was a grand plan written somewhere, 'Tom and Angela, love at first sight until death parts them.' Yeah, right." She wiped her hands on her apron, creamy white with the A Taste for All Pleasures logo Bonnie designed in rich burgundy: various breads tumbling from a cornucopia. "Death didn't part us, his dick did."

Bonnie gave a shout of laughter, then clapped her hand over her mouth.

"I'm sorry." Her fingers lifted to let the words out. "It's not funny, except that it is."

"I know. It's funny now. Sort of. Sometimes." Angela wrinkled her nose. "I just don't know how you ever trust that love-feeling again once you've been busted up like this."

"You want to know what I think?" Bonnie's walnut-chunk

was fast disappearing. "I think someday you'll meet a guy who makes you realize how effed-up Tom was. You didn't have anyone to compare him to since he was your first love."

Angela stared at her, wondering if she had any idea how that advice could be applied to herself about Seth. Probably not. Every time Angela gently broached the subject of Mr. Can't-Commit, Bonnie turned bristly with denial and stopped listening. "You may be right. But forgive me if I am not holding my breath."

"Understandable. We all have to go through our bitter stage." She started backing out, hand raised in a wave worthy of royalty. "I've gotta get back to the store. Thanks for the cookies."

"You're welcome. Thanks for the bouquet." Angela watched her scoot over to her shop, worrying that there hadn't been enough flower-selling going on lately if Bonnie's frequent drop-ins to the bakery were any indication. It wasn't easy starting your own business; the five of them had some pretty rough times just getting the building bought and renovated. Close friendship was the miracle that helped them survive, but none were taking long-term success for granted.

They'd passed the one-year anniversary of the building's grand opening three months earlier, in January. They'd named the collection of businesses Come to Your Senses after one of them—Bonnie, Angela thought realized that their five fields represented the five senses: taste—Angela's bakery; sound—Seth's music; smell—Bonnie's flowers; sight—Jack's photography; and touch—Caroline's physical therapy studio, bought by a woman named Demi Anderson after their beloved friend got married and moved out of state. The building's sign, painted in whimsical, colorful letters by Bonnie, hung over the front entrance to the ornate brick building on the corner of Broadway and Olive, a great location surrounded by other businesses, with Seattle Central Community College and Cal Anderson Park a few blocks down the street, and with nearby neighborhoods housing a population that wholeheartedly embraced the concept of anything goes.

The door chimed—another customer, or in this case, a slew of them, teenagers ready for a pre-dinner appetite spoiler. Angela called Scott, her black-haired multipierced part-time student helper, out of the back where he was sweeping the kitchen, and together they got the crowd taken care of. Two tangerine scones, three pumpkin muffins, eight assorted cookies and four cupcakes. Nothing from France: mille-feuilles, croissants. Nothing from Greece: baklava, kourambiedes. Nothing from Italia: pignoli cookies, spumenti, each recipe made with her own special twist.

Scott returned to his sweeping and Angela glared around the now-empty shop, the last coffee-drinker having vacated his table. She was not going to give up her dream of having a bakery like the ones she and Tom saw on their European honeymoon. Especially because Tom's voice was still echoing in her head—*stick with what you can manage*—as if he'd never expected her to rise above a chocolate chip cookie. As if she'd always be plain old unsophisticated Angie...

Stalking out into the store, armed with a rag and cleaner, she wiped down the four small and rather rickety tables. Someday her bakery would be the talk of the town. Not for bran and bland, but for elegant and exotic. She'd be—

"Excuse me."

Angela turned abruptly. Customer. She hadn't heard the chime? It meant a lot to her when people first entered the shop to be waiting attentively, welcoming smile in place. "Hi, there. May I help you?"

Oh, my goodness. *Oh, my goodness.* Had they opened the gates to Olympus and shooed a demigod into her shop?

Clear blue eyes. Strong chin. Sandy hair, kept short. Golden skin. Mouth with clean lines, slightly fuller lower lip—she must be staring like a crazy person to notice all that.

And he was staring back. Expectantly. Had he answered her offer of help? Had she missed that, too? Had she gone suddenly deaf?

She scooted to safety behind the counter to stash the cleaner and regain her composure, then tried again. "May I help you find something?"

"Oh. Sorry. Yeah." He laughed awkwardly, a surprising contrast to the masculine-warrior aura he gave off. "I guess I was in another world."

Whew. So she wasn't the one who had taken that trip. "I understand. Sometimes this world is hard to take."

He looked wary, as if he thought she were about to recommend a specific alternative. "Very true."

Silence.

She could not ask him *again* what he wanted. So she'd stand here gazing her fill while he scanned the cases until he figured it out. Now that she looked past the initial impression of "hot damn," she saw his eyes were haunted, dark circles under them; a vertical line bisected his brows; the stunning lips were set tightly. Not a happy man.

As usual, when she encountered someone in pain, Angela wanted to help. Stuffing a person with baked goods wasn't always a healthy way to deal with grief, but sometimes short-term sweetness went a long way toward curing what ailed a person.

"If you have any questions…"

"I *am* here to buy something, not just to stand gawking." He tore his eyes away from her bread shelf, mouth quirked in a self-deprecating smile that didn't reach his eyes, but softened his features enough that Angela's heart skipped a beat. Not so much the wounded warrior when he smiled. More like a man she'd like to get to know. As a friend. A very sexy friend…

"All gawkers welcome." She returned his smile, feeling as if some internal light fixture, which had been dark for ages, was sparking signs of life. "Did you have something in mind?"

"Yes, actually."

"Bread?" She gestured to the loaves he'd been ogling. "All made daily on the premises."

"No, actually." His voice broke. "I'm here for cupcakes."

Cupcakes. So much emotion in that word. What was the significance? She was dying to ask, but gestured instead to the case on her right, where rows of them, somewhat depleted by the day's purchases, were displayed. Angela decided impulsively that this particular demigod was a chocolate guy. Not devil's food or German sweet, but dense, moist, bittersweet. Possibly with coffee frosting, or caramel, but more likely chocolate sour cream. "Flavor?"

"White with white frosting."

No. No way. She was so sure, she found herself having to stop from shaking her head at him. White-on-white? He didn't get that lean, muscular body by inhaling sugar. That lean muscular body, which she had noticed keenly, was displayed to advantage in a tight athletic shirt. Below the counter she could glimpse black biking shorts hugging powerful thighs. In large, strong-looking hands he held a biking helmet.

Times like these she was very glad her cases were see-through.

"White-on-white?" She put her hands on her hips, regarded him doubtfully. "I would have said chocolate."

"Yes, usually." He glanced at the chocolate flavors, then back to her, causing a renewed buzz in her internal circuitry. "Today white."

"A gift?"

"Sort of."

"Special occasion?"

"Birthday." His words became clipped, lips thinning.

Angela nodded, wanting nothing more than to continue her

interrogation, but recognizing the signal to back off. "How many would you like?"

"Six."

"Six white-on-white coming up." She grabbed a flat box and pulled it into shape. "Is it your birthday?"

"No." He spoke as if he were strangling on the word.

Hmm. She glanced at him after the first cupcake, feather-light under clouds of sweet icing, had gone into the box. She wasn't going to pry if it made him uncomfortable, but she wished there was something she could do or say to help. Tom's very sensible voice spoke again in her brain—*Why are you always wasting energy taking on problems that aren't yours?* Yes, yes, he was right. But…

"Would you like a chocolate cupcake for yourself right now? On the house?"

"I'd…" He frowned, seeming to deliberate. "No. No, thanks."

As if he were tempted, but shouldn't. Diabetic maybe? With a bod like that he certainly couldn't be concerned about losing weight. Whomever's birthday he was celebrating with cupcakes he didn't care for must have power over him. Though he didn't look like the kind of man a woman could dominate.

Listen to her. She knew nothing about this guy and was already inventing an overbearing girlfriend and hating her. It could just as easily be true that his woman was a total sweetheart and he was a rat bastard who'd done her wrong. Cupcakes could be his way of trying to squirm back into her good graces.

"I'm Angela by the way." She put the fourth cupcake in the box.

"Oh." He looked confused. Then wary again. "Uh, hi."

Not going to tell her his name apparently. Angela put cupcakes five and six in the box, slighted by the rejection. "You live around here?"

"Not far."

She glanced pointedly at the helmet, feeling reckless now. The guy didn't want to talk to her? Too bad. She wanted to talk to him. And until he got what he'd come in for, he was her prisoner. "You ride a lot? On all these hills? Our neighborhood has some of the city's worst."

"Biking clears my head."

Cleared his head. That was progress. Practically an intimate confession. "Your head needed clearing today?"

He blinked, eyes losing their blankness and fixing on her vividly. "Something like that."

The old sputtering bulb inside her started a steady glow. This man was truly delicious. His combination of ultramacho body and vulnerable demeanor...

Apparently she was a sucker for a fixer-upper.

Her demigod gave the boxed cupcakes a pointed glance.

Right. She started to close the lid, then hesitated. White frosting, white cake, white box, bleah. "Would you like these gift-wrapped?"

"No, I'll just take them."

She frowned. For whatever reason she wanted to give him something with color. "Even a ribbon?"

"No, not a ribbon, nothing. It's fine as is." He spoke calmly, wasn't impatient, which gave her courage to look up again.

Their eyes met and held, and her heart gave a lurch of sympathy and, yes, attraction. He looked half-broken, and even more masculine for the pain.

He looked away first; Angela picked up the box, cheeks flushing. The last man she'd been instantly drawn to like this was Tom, and look what poison he'd turned out to be. Though Tom's look had been cocky, sexual, beckoning. The haunted look in this man's eyes was entirely different. And much more powerful.

"I'll be right back." She fled to the back of the shop,

grabbed one of the overflow chocolate-on-chocolate cup-cakes, wrapped it in bright red paper and tucked it neatly in the center of the box, which she tied with a length of rainbow ribbon.

Maybe he wouldn't appreciate the gesture. Maybe she was spoiling some birthday surprise for a woman he loved, maybe he'd come back furious and cause a scene. Maybe. But this guy was miserable, and he wasn't a white-cake eater, and Angela wanted to give him something that might also make him smile.

More than that, after he left her shop, got on his bike and pedaled away, she wanted him to have something that would remind him of her.

2

DANIEL FLYNN climbed the newly carpeted stairs to his second-floor apartment, carrying his bike in one hand, his riding bag with the box of cupcakes in the other. At the landing, he rolled his eyes at the new gold and ivory cherub figurines his landlord apparently decided would look good on the windowsill, and kept climbing, legs leaden and shaky after his thirty-mile ride on Seattle's hilly streets. A longer ride than usual, but he'd been in one of his self-punishing moods, trying to use physical pain to squelch the emotional.

Today was Kate's birthday, exactly two months before his. She would have been twenty-nine. She would have completed her first year of graduate school and be into her second. They would have been getting married in six months, right after she graduated.

Over and over, around and around, like a merry-go-round made of spikes, the emotions tore into him as they had for the past year. Granted, in the last few months there had been minutes, then hours, then finally whole days that were easier here and there, and the intensity of the pain had lessened on the whole, but significant occasions like today brought his Kate roaring back, her image, spirit, even her scent...*her*. How could he ever get over someone who was so much a part of him? The final stage of grief was supposed to be acceptance. Did that mean at some point a loss like this would be okay with him? Impossible. Kate had become the anchor of his world from the moment he met her when they were both at Highland Park High School outside Chicago. They'd started dating almost immediately, and in her he'd found all the love and stability his feuding parents were too busy to remember he needed. Without her, he would have taken a seriously self-destructive turn in order to cope.

Outside the bachelor apartment he shared with his coworker, Jake, he set the bike down, grimacing at the volume of music coming through the door. Coldplay. Not his favorite. He fumbled in the zipped pocket of his bag for his key, feeling the sharp corner of the bakery box inside. Kate's weakness, white cupcakes with white frosting, the more sugary the better. Daniel had always been a chocolate guy. Funny how the woman at the store guessed that. She'd seemed very perceptive. Her eyes—beautiful eyes, brown and widely spaced, friendly and bright—had seemed to peer right inside him.

Daniel's fingers touched the key, closed around it and held still. She'd had nice hair, too, brown with reddish tints, cascading and shiny, falling from a widow's peak at the crown of her wide, pale forehead. Odd how he remembered her so vividly. The quick smile, the cheerful energy she brought to her movements…

He drew out the key abruptly and jammed it into the lock. Today, he'd honor Kate's memory by eating the treats she loved. Earlier he'd also bought the ingredients for her favorite meal: rib-eye steak, creamed spinach and brown and wild rices mixed together, though right now the idea of eating made his stomach churn. Small wonder he'd dropped nearly ten pounds in the past year and a half.

Inside, he wheeled his bike through their front hallway into his bedroom and leaned it against the wall, which was already marred with scuff marks from previous handlebar encounters. He dug out the cupcake box from his bag, and yanked his empty water bottle from its cage on the bike, feeling restless, grimy and stuck in a cage himself, from which the ride had liberated him only temporarily. The small apartment with gray carpet and his room with bare, white walls—his own fault for not hanging pictures—didn't help.

A shower got rid of the grime, but didn't help his mood. Pounding on Jake's door quieted the music, but underscored the painful fact: some days he just had to get through. Luckily Jake understood. The two men had met at Slatewood International, where they designed software to stay ahead of increasingly sophisticated hackers, and had formed a fast friendship. After Kate's accident, Jake had been solid, taking Daniel in, and developing an uncanny sense of when to kid him out of a scowl and when to back off, when to prod him into talking and when to leave him alone.

Sometimes Daniel felt he owed Jake his sanity—however much of it he still had left. Kate would approve. Sort of. She and Jake got along like fire and ice. She thought Jake was a shallow butthead; he thought Kate was an uptight bitch. Daniel had sat in the middle, rolling his eyes at both of them.

In the kitchen, he pulled the steak out of the refrigerator to warm up, and put the brown-and-wild rice mixture on the stove to cook. Daniel was a bread man, always preferred it to rice or potatoes, preferably fresh the way it had looked at Angela's bakery, thick slices spread with softened butter.

Did she get up early every morning and make it herself? He pictured her, drawn-back hair emphasizing her heart-shaped face, flour dusting her high cheekbones, room warm with the fresh, yeasty smell of dough.

But tonight, for Kate, he'd eat rice.

With leaden movements, he pulled down the bottle of her favorite Washington State cabernet from Donedei vineyards, got out the fancy corkscrew she'd bought him and hesitated. Before he met Kate, he'd been a beer guy, and reverted to being one after her death, since he associated wine so strongly with their relationship.

The bottle went back up on the shelf for another, easier day. Too many triggers. Fine line between honoring her memory and needlessly torturing himself. Kate of all people would understand. He opened the refrigerator, grabbed out a Mack & Jack's Serengeti Wheat beer and felt himself relax a little.

"Hey." Jake ambled into the kitchen and gestured at the steak. "Nice piece of meat. What's the occasion?"

"Kate's birthday." He answered automatically, robotically. "Her favorite meal."

"Oh. Yeah, um. Okay." Frowning, he grabbed a beer, popped off the top and took a long swig. "So. How are you doing on all that?"

Daniel took a long swig himself, wanting to laugh at the perfect sitcom moment. Two guys drinking beer, trying to talk about emotions. "Okay."

"You're celebrating her birthday tonight." His tone made it clear he thought the idea was beyond moronic. Jake was not exactly the sentimental type. "You gonna eat that all yourself?"

Daniel shrugged. "Unlikely."

"Excellent." Jake pulled up a chair to the table in their bland kitchen, gray on white on black. "You have yourself a dinner date."

"I guess I do." Not exactly his plan, but now that Jake was here, the idea of sitting alone miserably thinking about Kate felt like a direct route to unnecessary pain, pain he was tired of having to battle.

"I met this girl last night."

"Yeah?" Daniel got up and grabbed a bag of pretzel twists from the counter, brought it back to the table. Jake had a genius for interacting with the opposite sex. Women found his puppy-dog dark eyes brimming with humor and short stocky body unthreatening. Before they knew it, he'd literally charmed the pants off of them. Few relationships lasted longer than a month or two, but Jake kept trying, claiming he'd eventually stumble over the great love his parents had. "How come you slept here last night, you strike out?"

"She's not for me." Jake tipped his beer bottle toward Daniel. "Your type. Brainy, petite, high-energy."

Daniel's grin faded abruptly. "You know I can't—"

"Yes, I know." He rolled his eyes and made his fingers "talk" like a sock puppet. "You promised Kate you wouldn't date until your wedding date, which, after a year and a half of celibacy is still six months away."

"Jake..." Daniel warned.

Jake put down his hand. "Cruel and unusual punishment."

"Punishment." Daniel chuckled bitterly, shaking his head. He and Kate had been looking toward their wedding day for so long, planning, dreaming, fantasizing. How could Daniel even think about another woman before that date had passed?

Okay, maybe he could think about other women. Once in a while. Like now, when Angela's luminous face had come into his head again. "You don't understand."

"Why wouldn't she leave it to *you* to decide when you were ready to move on? Wouldn't you know better than she would?"

Daniel narrowed his eyes, tamping down the instant flash of temper. "Lay off Kate."

"Someone needs to say this shit, Daniel. She had you by the testicles while she was alive, now you're moping around like you buried your balls with her." He leaned forward, eyes earnest, dark hair falling forward, in spite of the gel he tried to keep it combed back with. "Dig 'em up, dude! Start living again! Go out with a woman, or two, or three. You're not being unfaithful, Kate is *gone*."

"I *know* she's gone." Daniel spoke through his teeth. "I feel it every day."

"Because you haven't tried to get past it."

Anger rose so fiercely Daniel had to white-knuckle his beer to keep from punching Jake in the mouth. "What the hell do you know about it?"

"Everything."

His answer shocked some of Daniel's anger out of him. "How?"

"My high school girlfriend. We dated three years. Aneurism. She was there—" he snapped his fingers "—then she wasn't. But you know what? That was her life ending. Mine went on."

"So you climbed on top of the next babe who came along and that fixed everything?"

"Yes, I did and no, it didn't. But dating after her death didn't mean I never loved her or that I didn't miss her. I still do sometimes. But I sure as hell didn't serve some bullshit two-year sentence crying over my dick in my own hand."

"Shut the f—"

"I'm telling you, you bury yourself in that shit, your life might as well be over, too."

"Stop." Daniel stood abruptly, chair scraping over the hardwood floor.

"Okay." Jake held up both hands. "Okay. Calm down."

"Don't ever say that crap about Kate again."

"Okay. I was out of line. I was *right,* but I was out of line."

Daniel stayed where he was, trying to get his breathing under control. Most of the time he believed strongly that people could think and say what they wanted, it was no skin off his ass. But Jake's words had cut deep. "You want this steak or not?"

"Sure, man." Jake nodded. "Sure. You need any help?"

"No." He turned to the stove and started a pan heating. By the time the steak was ready to be turned, he'd calmed down some. After they'd finished it—Daniel had more appetite than he expected, and the steak was damn good—he was tired of Jake's apologetically cheerful conversation, and just wanted to retreat to his room and reconnect with Kate over the cupcakes.

"I'm going out with Mark tonight. You want to come?"

"No, thanks." Daniel took his plate to the dishwasher.

"Do you good. Take your mind off the bad stuff."

"I'm staying in."

Jake shrugged. "Okay. Your choice."

"Yeah, how about that."

Jake chuckled. "I won't say another word."

"I doubt that."

"Not tonight anyway." He put his own plate in the dishwasher and slapped Daniel on the back. "It gets better."

"So I hear."

"And it will get better a lot faster if you—" He saw the look on Daniel's face and backed up, hands lifted again. "Right. I'm going. I'm gone."

A few minutes later the kitchen was clean, the front door closed behind Jake. Daniel went into his room with the cupcakes and put on Kate's favorite CD, *Little Earthquakes* by Tori Amos.

The music filled the room, poignant and throaty, gut-wrenchingly evocative. Daniel drifted back toward the desk, throat thickening, remembering Kate singing along, horribly out of tune, which had grated on his nerves. The memory seemed so endearing now. In a trance, he carefully untied the burgundy and gold ribbons he hadn't wanted on the box and lifted the lid.

What the—

Chocolate. There was a chocolate cupcake nestled in red paper in the center of the white ones he'd asked for, devil amidst the angels. *Angela.* Her face rose in his mind again, pretty mouth curved in a smile, eyes brimming with mischief as she handed him the box after her mysterious disappearance into the back room.

The tiniest burst of light skittered through his chest. He found himself half smiling. Angela had guessed he was a chocolate guy, and made sure he got what she was so sure he'd like. The gesture was a little weird. But also…oddly sweet.

The light in his chest burst again. She'd been tall, as he remembered. Maybe five-seven or five-eight. Kate had been tiny, five-three to his six feet two inches, but with wiry strength that continually astounded him. Any and all obstacles buckled from the sheer force of Kate's determination.

And she'd been determined he not date until their wedding day had passed. Her last wish, whispered as her young, promising life left her. Daniel had been so devastated he would have promised her anything.

He pulled up his desk chair and sat, rubbing his hands on his jean-clad thighs. He could smell the chocolate, wafting up like temptation from the innocent vanilla surrounding it.

His finger swiped through rich, dark frosting, lifted it to his mouth.

Ohh, man. Real chocolate, killer chocolate. Bitter and sweet, with a tang of some kind—sour cream?

He tried the white frosting.

Mmm. Cleanly sweet with an appealing vanilla-marshmallow flavor. Fresh, real ingredients there, too.

His hand went back down on his thigh. He pictured Kate in the hospital, head raised painfully toward him, her pretty features bruised, contorting with the effort to speak. *No other women until after our wedding day. Please. Do that for me. And for you. For us…*

Throat on fire with the impossible task of trying to choke back tears, he'd answered in a voice that barely sounded. *Yes. I promise.*

In his lonely room now, the first song ended. The next one came on.

He saw himself suddenly through Jake's eyes, spending

the evening alone in his room, listening to music he wouldn't have chosen, about to eat food he didn't much care for.

Daniel shook his head. It was Kate's birthday. He was honoring her. Tomorrow he'd think about what Jake had said. But tonight…

If you bury yourself in that shit, your life might as well be over, too.

I would definitely have pegged you for a chocolate guy.

His hand hesitated over the box.

Kate…

He dug out a cupcake, peeled off the paper and took a huge bite, with more enthusiasm than he'd had for any food in a long, long time.

The cupcake was as amazing as the frosting, light but moist, and incredibly flavorful. The best he'd ever had. Or maybe it was the release and relief of letting himself enjoy it.

The beautiful fresh-faced Angela had been right. Tonight he'd been ready for chocolate.

3

"She'll love them." Bonnie handed over a bouquet of mixed blue, purple and yellow to the grinning teenage boy who'd come in and dubiously asked for roses, but was leaving much happier. Bonnie had listened to his tale with sympathy: he'd been peer-pressured into asking The Wrong Girl to the homecoming dance, then realized he really cared for The Right Girl all along, and wanted a gesture of combined apology and affection that wasn't too intense or expensive....

Sometimes Bonnie thought she was more of a psychologist than a saleswoman. People might tell hairdressers more of their troubles, but they'd be surprised how many emotions went along with flowers. Not just wedding, funeral, birthday and anniversary. Also apology, seduction, guilt, renewal...

Bonnie was a firm believer in the healing powers of floral arrangements. Maybe that sounded crazy, but she'd seen it over and over again, customers coming back in to thank her, telling her how much the plants or bouquets or blossoms had been appreciated, how they'd helped cheer or heal, intensify or diffuse.

She wiped water drops off her counter and leaned on it, surveying the riot of fresh color around her proudly and a little wistfully. Proud, because she hadn't wanted her stock isolated away from the customer, refrigerated behind glass; her flowers bloomed all over the store in buckets carefully arranged on multiple levels as to color and size. The effect, she hoped, was like walking into an English garden in full bloom. Wistful, because not enough people had been walking in, to the point where she was having to consider drastic measures. Not selling the store, not yet, but…yes, drastic. Like giving up her apartment upstairs and dragging essentials and a cot into the shop's back office.

After a year of lukewarm sales, she was getting to where she needed to be realistic and face the possibility of failure. In the meantime, she was looking around for marketing tips, tricks and gimmicks wherever she could get them, hoping to find ways of luring in more buyers. And constantly fighting off panic and a heavy sense of doom…and of shame.

Just another super fun year in the game of life.

Through her window onto the building's foyer she noticed a guy dressed in biking gear, and holding a helmet walk in and stop, as if he weren't sure where to go. Bonnie frowned. He looked familiar. Where had she seen him?

Aha. *Déjà vu.* She'd seen him pause in the same spot the previous day. Hard to miss a hard-body hottie like that. But when she'd glimpsed his face, she'd wanted less to seduce him than to offer hugs and mugs of coffee, maybe give him an air fern from her shop, so he wouldn't have to take care of anything but himself.

She craned her neck to get a better view. He was still hesitating. Maybe she should ask if he needed help? Yesterday he'd gone into Angela's. Bonnie meant to ask her about him, but A Taste for All Pleasures had been crazy busy and then Angela had gone out with friends last night.

A group of students, on a weekend break from classes, came out of the bakery, clutching paper bags of treats and cups of coffee. Hard-body Hottie stood aside to let them pass, then walked, without hesitation this time, into the bakery.

Ooh, interesting. Waiting to go in until Angela was alone? Bonnie hoisted herself onto her counter and leaned over shamelessly to catch Angela's reaction. A nice, wide smile, her usual greeting. But maybe this smile was wider? Nicer? Bonnie leaned farther, but couldn't see the guy's face. Was he after the buns or the baker? And would Angela let him taste the latter along with the former? Bonnie would love to see Angela happy again after that jerk ex of hers. Though they'd all fallen for Tom. He was impossible not to love, until you sensed the dry rot in his soul.

"Spy alert."

Bonnie nearly fell off her counter. "Damn it, Seth, you scared me to death."

"What did I miss?" Seth Blackstone sauntered up to her, grinning, making her shop look all the more colorful and feminine next to his tall, black-clad, self-assured masculinity. "Hot times at Angela's?"

"She's got a cute guy in there."

"Yeah?" He peered toward the bakery. "What's she doing with him?"

"Talking." Bonnie told her heartbeat to calm down. It was Seth, not the Pope.

"You know this guy?"

"No. But he was in yesterday, and she seemed glad to see him."

"Angela's glad to see everyone." He leaned against Bonnie's counter, poked at her neat pile of brochures until they fanned to one side. "She's a sweetheart."

"True." Bonnie sighed and jumped down behind her counter again. "I'd love to see her dating."

"Why would you wish something like that on a friend?"

"Ha. Ha." She turned a withering glare on him, which threatened to melt into a giggle at the smiling mischief in his hazel eyes. Oh, those eyes. Narrow and fiercely masculine, as was the strong square set of his jaw. But she couldn't start thinking that way again. She'd keep up the prickly banter—it seemed the only way they could get along was by constantly disagreeing. So she glanced at her watch, maintaining the frown of disapproval. "Well, look at that. Nearly time for lunch. You just out of bed?"

"Ha. I'll have you know I've been up for hours." He took her wrist and turned it so he could see the time. "Okay, hour."

Bonnie snatched back her arm as if his touch annoyed her, when five years after this man broke off their junior-year romance and smashed her heart, he could still make her shiver. Somewhere along the way she'd managed to make uneasy peace with the fact that she'd most likely always feel something for Seth, even having dated other men since then. The trick was keeping those emotions under control so they didn't ruin her friendship with him or her sanity. Or, God forbid, screw up the perfectly balanced friend-dynamics of the owners of Come to Your Senses.

"What's new?" She straightened a group of pencils, picked up the brochures and tapped them on the counter, aware the busy work would look as ridiculous as it was.

"Got a possible job with an independent director who needs a film scored."

"Really!" Bonnie grinned at his look of utter indifference, seeing straight through to the celebration going on inside him. Seth might hold secrets for most people, but he held few for her and she still treasured that.

She was happy for him. His piano studio seemed to be thriving, and he'd been getting good commercial work, too. Not that he needed the income—the Blackstones had made a fortune many times over, starting with great-great-grand-father Blackstone's shipping company right there in Seattle. But to Seth's credit, he didn't sit back and spend family money. He'd been actively pursuing his passion, striving for a career in the music business—songwriting, scoring commercials and/or films, and teaching piano.

"So what's going on with you?" He squinted at her. "You look like hell."

"Oh, you are so sweet!" She shoved at him, then immediately wished she hadn't. That place in the center of his chest, the flat plane between the hard swells of his pectoral muscles, where dark hair curled—she missed that place, as if it were a whole person. Missed pillowing her head there, missed stroking, kissing, biting, the scent of his skin.

Yikes. She was being extra sappy and nostalgic today, what was with that? Reigniting those particular embers of passion was about as smart as playing tag on the highway. She had more important things to think about than the sternum of a guy who dumped her.

Most likely the new-old feelings were a result of extra vulnerability over her business, and missing the steady support of a romantic partner. Perfectly understandable when times got rough.

Well, guess what? Seth's support might have been steady at first, but as Bonnie had started feeling more comfortable mentioning the future, Seth had started drawing back, further and further until he bumped into a surgically enhanced bimbo and stuck there.

"You still with me? I asked why you look so terrible." He hadn't taken his eyes off her, eyes that showed real concern. Worse, when she shoved against his chest again, he took her hand and held onto it. "Seriously, Bon-bon, what is it? Something's really bugging you. Has been for a while."

She shrugged, hating his sympathy and the way it still made her want to melt. "What makes you think that?"

"You've lost weight. You're holding your body tense. You have dark shadows under your eyes and that worry-groove going full-force." He traced a line from the center of her forehead between her brows. "Right here."

Bonnie held her breath, telling herself his touch meant

nothing, that Seth practiced charm on women the same way most people used oxygen: involuntarily and 24/7.

"I'm fine." She held his gaze defiantly. "Great, in fact."

"Good." His face turned stony and he pushed away from the counter. "Glad to hear it."

And there they stood on opposite sides of their post-relationship chasm. He kept pushing and she wouldn't give him the satisfaction of intimacy without…intimacy. Though damn it, he hadn't spoken to her with that much tenderness since before they broke up. Hadn't used her "Bon-bon" nickname in quite a while, either.

So! She should call Greg, the last guy she dated, whom she'd broken up with amicably, to see if he wanted to hang out. Maybe in bed. She needed to shake both this silly renewed vulnerability to Seth and her dark mood over Bonnie Blooms.

"Ah, here she is." Seth turned abruptly and strode out into the wide corridor outside her entranceway.

Bonnie followed him with her eyes, which had the enjoyable task of watching him greet a woman with obvious affection. Not just any woman. Not a woman Bonnie could look at and think, "Oh, how nice, Seth is meeting a good friend." No. This was one of those women men dream about having their whole lives. And thank God Bonnie knew Seth well enough not to have unbent just now, not to have leaned on him, not to have let him back under her skin even the tiniest fraction of an inch, or she'd be feeling humiliated and rejected. Again.

Seth caught the goddess's hand and pulled her into the shop after him. "Hey, Bonnie, this is my friend Alexandra."

Of course it was Alexandra, which he pronounced Alex-*ahn*-drah. Names like Matilda or Priscilla were entirely out of the question. She was tall, exotically dark, Selma Hayek-ish, wearing a dress—black cap sleeves, red lace-up corset and a black tutu skirt—over stiletto boots, and not looking at all stupid. Looking, in fact, like the Goddess of Fashion

Elegance. If Bonnie put on an outfit like that people would fall over laughing in the street.

Goddess looked eagerly around and parted her beautiful mouth to exclaim, "Oh, what a great shop!"

Bonnie suppressed a chortle of satisfaction. Alex-*ahn*-drah's voice brought to mind angry chipmunks. See? No one could have everything. Though this woman did have an unfair number of the characteristics particularly dear to Seth. Namely big boobs and long legs.

"Ooh!" Alexa glided—yes, glided—on heels that would make Bonnie walk as if she were drunk, over to the bucket of cut jasmine sprays, where she bent down to sniff. "These are sooo pretty! And they smell sooo nice."

"They're one of my favorites." In a faintly bitchy gesture, she made her voice as smooth and throatily sexual as possible, and got a satisfying double take from Seth.

"How much are they?" Alexandra bit her lower lip anxiously.

"Allow me." Seth plucked out several stems and handed them to Bonnie, not taking his eyes off of Alexandra's assets.

"Oh, wow. Thank you, Seth," the Goddess squeaked. "Those are so beautiful."

"How about roses, too? Red?"

"You are just too nice. Those would be *perfect*."

Seth turned to Bonnie, chest puffed like a knight who'd just rescued his lady. "We'll take these and a couple of—"

"Yeah, I'm on it." She was already heading for the red roses, rolling her eyes. She'd been standing three feet away. Did they think she couldn't hear?

Still gritting her teeth, she arranged the jasmine and roses with greenery and wrapped the bouquet while Seth led Alexandra around the shop and got to hear her chipmunking over everything. Bonnie wanted to charge him triple. He and

Bambi were probably on their way to his studio to make beautiful music together. Nice of him to flaunt that in front of her.

No. No. She took a deep breath. Another one. *Seriously, Bonnie...think.*

Seth didn't owe her that kind of consideration after five years. Not his fault he didn't know she couldn't quite put out the lame torch she still carried for him. Bonnie couldn't punish him for moving on to live his life the way he wanted, or for assuming she'd done the same.

She'd tried to move on. Truly. And in many important ways she had. But what had made her believe junior year with all her naive little heart that she and Seth were meant to be together was the way he opened up to her, the way he became unguarded and warm around her. Only her. The way they shared stories, sometimes vulnerable painful stories, about their origins and paths, noting how many of the emotions and the resulting damage were the same in spite of their radically different backgrounds. Seth's parents had been too caught up in their globe-trotting and social life to spend time with him, and Bonnie's were too busy just trying to cope with six kids and a mortgage.

Similar as their experiences had been, as adults they processed the reaction differently, and that was where she felt she could be the most help to him. Bonnie had craved the intimacy she'd been starved for during her childhood, surrounding herself with close friends and lovers. Seth had withdrawn into his music and let only a few trusted friends near him, but no one ever as close as she'd gotten during that blissful year they were together.

"Here you go." She handed the flowers to Alex-*ahn*-dra with a warm smile, determined not to act the pathetic hanger-on ex-girlfriend.

"Thanks." Alexandra buried her perfect nose in the bouquet and sent Seth a whitened smile under eyes glistening with gratitude. "Really, thank you."

"You're welcome." Sir Galahad's voice oozed humble nobility.

Bonnie was ready to hurl into one of her buckets.

"Ready?" Seth put a hand to the spot on Alexandra's back where the red corset met the sudden flare of black netting, and gestured toward the exit. They left together, Seth sending Bonnie an unreadable glance as they passed. She watched them go, unable to keep herself from hoping they'd turn left, head out of the building and into the city.

They turned right. Maybe to pay a visit to Jack's photography studio down the hall? Or Demi's physical therapy studio?

Bonnie came out from behind the counter and nonchalantly strolled toward a potted ficus, which she examined closely for yellowing leaves, keeping the couple in her peripheral vision through the line of windows across her storefront.

Her heart sank. No. They were waiting for the elevator. Going up to Seth's apartment.

She turned and stalked back to her counter. That was it. Bonnie could not spend the rest of her life skulking around ficuses spying on a guy who broke her heart *five years* earlier and hadn't shown any sign of any desire or even awareness that he had the power to change into someone looking for a serious, healthy relationship.

How many times had she told herself she had to let him go? Too many. This time she had to dig down really deep, face really hard truths and make damn well sure she meant it.

4

ANGELA SMILED AT the group of moms leaving her shop, laughing and chatting, pushing babies in strollers, holding sticky hands of cookie-finishing toddlers. Adorable. If she and Tom were still married, Angela would probably be pregnant by now. They'd wanted kids, boatloads of them, but had decided to wait a few years before trying—thank goodness. Maybe he'd have that boatload now with the Princess of Perfection.

The thought still managed to hurt.

It shouldn't. Tom was not worthy. Angela would meet someone else, someone who wanted her for herself, not in order to rebel against his parents. She and Mr. Wonderful would have perfectly flawed children and a perfectly flawed marriage like real, perfectly flawed people were supposed to.

Of course to do that, she'd have find Mr. Wonderful, and to do that, she'd have to start dating. Yesterday when she told Bonnie she wasn't ready, for the first time the response had felt more like reflex than truth. Angela had lain in bed last night and thought about how when the sexy bicycle guy came in for white cupcakes, she'd felt not just ready, she'd felt ex-*treme*-ly ready. Ready to drag him into the back and show him how hot her ovens could get. So maybe it was time to start? Maybe. She could always take refuge in delay if the reality proved even more terrifying than the thought. Just because Bike Guy happened to send her to the moon and back didn't mean she was ready for a relationship. After such a spectacular failure with her marriage it would be hard to trust any man again.

The pack of moms cleared the entrance and Angela's eyes snapped into focus on the devil himself. She did a cartoonish double take, her system burning with that exhausting and all-too-familiar combination of pain, anger and lingering tenderness.

Tom.

What was he doing here?

He looked good. He'd lost weight, had color, probably from a vacation with what's-er-name in St. Thomas, his favorite destination. Had he made love to her out on the warm sand at sundown? Watched the stars come out, more than Angela had ever seen before? Had the cooling air washed over their naked bodies? Did he tell her she was and always would be the only woman for him?

Angela wanted to cry. And she wanted to find a large blunt object to brain him with.

Divorce was so peaceful.

"Hi, Ange."

There was nothing she hated more than the sound of that nickname on his lips. "Hi, Tom. I'm surprised to see you."

"Yeah, well." He looked around, dark eyes taking in her shop, the tables and chairs she'd bought secondhand and painted black and burgundy herself, the counter and stools, the display cases of pastry, cakes and cookies, the racks of bread and rolls. Angela found herself holding her breath, awaiting his judgment, and told herself to grow a pair. What did she care what he thought?

Too much. Much too much. She could not wait for the day when he no longer mattered, when his opinion was so much blah-blah-blah fouling the air. Three years since they divorced. How much longer would she have to wait?

"Nice place." He nodded, hands perching on his hips. "You've done well."

Ah, there it was, the royal seal of approval. She hated herself for even the small swell of pleasure. "Thanks. Did you want something?"

"I came to talk to you. But while I'm here…" He stepped closer to the case, examining the neatly arranged goods, which Angela was satisfied to note had been healthily depleted by a solid Saturday morning of business.

She walked a few steps to her left and gestured proudly to the assortment of international pastries. Here was someone who'd definitely appreciate what she'd done. "Would you like to try an éclair? These are filled with chocolate lavender pastry cream. Those there with hazelnut coffee cream and cocoa nubs. Or I have black-pepper fruit tarts, passionfruit—"

"I'll try an éclair. Chocolate lavender. And a chocolate chunk cookie." He reached for his wallet and she waved him off.

"My treat. You want a box?"

"I'll eat them now." He patted his stomach. "Annabel and I are training for a triathlon this summer. I can manage the calories."

Triathlon. Of course. The Princess was in perfect shape, too. Angela would rather walk on live coals.

"You look great." She picked out the prettiest éclair and put it on an extra round of waxed paper and a napkin before handing it to him. Tom had a horror of getting his hands sticky.

"Thanks. I don't have you around to tempt me with bakery stuff anymore. It's been easy keeping the weight down."

Ah, there it was. His weight problem had been *her* fault. "Annabel isn't a cook?"

"We go out most of the time."

"Nice." He loved going out. Some evenings Angela had practically begged him to stay in. What kind of married couple ignored life at home?

It was good he found someone who fit him better.

There. That was about as charitable as she could be right now. Someday she'd do better.

"Not bad." He was chewing his first bite of éclair. "Interesting taste."

Interesting. That wasn't quite the rapturous response she'd hoped for. "Did you come for something other than calories?"

"Yeah." He wiped his fingers on the napkin. "Is there somewhere we could talk?"

"We're not talking now?" They were alone in the shop. Scott wasn't due for another half hour. Alice was back in the kitchen finishing a batch of baguette dough. Angela didn't want Tom in the tiny intimacy of her office.

"Okay." He took another huge bite of éclair. When he ate like that, as if he'd been starving for weeks, it meant he was nervous. Whatever Tom had to say, he didn't think she'd like hearing it. She didn't, either.

"You know Annabel and I have been dating for a while…"

"You're getting married." Pain shot through her. She-succeeded-where-I-failed pain, which was infuriatingly irrational. Not like Angela would *ever* want Tom back.

"Yes." He wolfed the rest of the éclair, wiped his fingers again and picked up the cookie while he was still chewing. "We're having a fall wedding."

"Congratulations, Tom. I'm happy for you." She was happy for him. And also still wanted that blunt object.

"I wouldn't blame you if you weren't. But I wanted you to hear it from me."

She nodded, managing to keep her gaze calm and steady. "That was nice of you, Tom."

It was nice. And nice to be reminded that there was a good

person inside somewhere, and that she hadn't been a total idiot marrying him.

Only three-quarters of one.

"Good. Well…" He bit into the cookie. She could feel his relief having gotten through that errand of mercy without having to endure a scene, and could feel his need to flee as soon as possible, having gotten through it. Fine by her.

"Thanks for coming by, Tom. I really—"

"Mmm." He held up the cookie, nearly halved by the size of the bite he'd taken. *"This* is where you should be focusing. This is your business's future. Leave the fancy stuff to someone who can really manage it, someone who really lives there. That's not you."

Somehow she kept the smile that had invited itself onto her features during his praise of the cookie. "I don't think—"

"Are you doing sales calls? Lots of them? Every day?"

Immediately she felt defensive. She hated sales calls, and while she knew they were important for growing her business, she tended to avoid them. Which he'd know, because he knew her, and because she wasn't answering his question right away. "I've done enough for me. I have a few restaur—"

"With these?" He held up the cookie.

"Right now I'm concentrating on the international pastry side of the bus—"

"Mistake. You're all-American and should stay in this country. Don't reach beyond yourself, Angie. You've always done that. You're doing it with this bakery, you did it by…" He stopped, looking trapped.

"Marrying you?"

"No. No, of course not." He shoved the rest of the cookie into his mouth, chewed furiously. "I didn't mean—"

"I know what you meant."

"No." He swallowed and sighed. "I don't think you do. We never could communicate. That was our problem."

Yeah, they had trouble communicating. He told her what

she should be like, and if she protested, he'd roll his eyes as if he'd been saddled with defective merchandise. When she did try to change, he'd cut down her every effort, exactly as he'd just done, with the result that she felt hopelessly inadequate through their relationship and short marriage. And was *still* working to get out from under the weight of his disapproval, damn him. And her.

"Well, I guess it's better we're not together anymore." She spoke flatly, struggling with anger and regret. "I hope Annabel will make you happy."

"Thanks, Ange." His features softened, he took a few steps toward her.

No, no hugging. *Go away.* "'Bye Tom! Have a great wedding!"

He took the hint, gave an awkward wave and left the shop.

Relief. More than relief—sudden satisfaction—because as she stared at his retreating figure, Angela noticed a hairless circle on the back of his head, perfectly natural, but something Tom had dreaded with near terror. Imagine that! Something in the world not obeying Tom Hulfish's wishes.

Angela managed a giggle and the giggle lightened her mood some. This was good. Recovery this soon after seeing him was a big step forward. Last time she'd bawled like a baby the minute his back was turned. This time she was only slightly shaky.

Progress.

She bent to pick up a dropped napkin; her doorbell sang out. A group of college kids, probably just awake, looking for breakfast at lunchtime. She served them, happy for further distraction. By the time they left, she was practically herself again—until she glanced out her door into the hallway beyond and for the second time that morning, did a double take.

The bike guy. Back. Striding into her shop. Looking severe.

Uh-oh. Was he going to yell at her about the chocolate cupcake? Tell her she'd ruined the perfect surprise he'd planned for a special lady?

That would suck.

She put on her usual welcoming smile, nerves making her mouth stretch with the effort, while the rest of her noted that he was still the hottest man she'd seen in a long, long time.

The hottest man she'd seen in a long, long time did something completely unexpected then. He smiled back.

Oh. My. The lingering emotions over the encounter with Tom were gone. Smashed. Obliterated.

In fact…Tom who?

The grin turned Bike Guy into a different person. Friendly. Boyish. Vital. And so sexy she practically had to grab for the counter to stay upright. Wind-tousled hair, light blue eyes, sexy indentations at the corners of his mouth, good strong chin with just the barest hint of a cleft…

"Hi, Angela."

"Hello…" She trailed pointedly, cuing him for his name.

"I got my cupcakes home last night. But…" He looked comically perplexed. "Apparently there was a mistake. I ordered six white-on-white and I got seven."

"Seven!?" She was all sweet innocence. Well, no, not all innocence. Just the parts he could see. "That is terrible."

"It gets worse. The seventh cupcake was chocolate."

"Chocolate." She faked astonishment, then frowned. "That's not like me, to get an order wrong. I'm pretty sure you're mistaken."

"No, mistake. Six white, one chocolate."

"I really don't think…" She narrowed her eyes. "Wait, what proof do you have? Pictures? A notarized statement? Crumbs?"

He put his hands to his hips, drawing attention—her attention anyway—to his broad chest. "The evidence has been tampered with. Destroyed. In fact, eaten."

"No evidence, case dismissed." She mimicked a gavel banging, then tipped her head to one side and realized with a thrill that he was fun as well as hot, and that she was flirting with him, which felt really, really good. "Did you enjoy it?"

"I did."

"Well, good." She gave a nod of satisfaction. "That's what you were supposed to do."

"Aha." He took a step toward the counter, blue eyes fixed on her. "You admit it."

She made herself look sweetly blank. "Admit what?"

Oh, it had been way, way too long since she'd done this. Her flirt muscles were unfurling, stretching, shaking off the dust. This was totally fun. Now she had to get Bonnie out flirting with her. Someone other than Seth.

"I came back to thank you." He pulled restlessly at the zipper on his bike shirt. "You were right. I'm a chocolate guy."

"I knew it." She smiled, wishing rather carnally that he'd yank the zipper all the way down, contenting herself instead with taking in the lean physique, displayed so beautifully in skin-tight, black, red and blue material. Tom might have lost weight, but next to this graceful Titan, his stocky build looked stunted.

"So how did the birthday boy, or—" she mixed a meaningful pause with a sidelong glance "—*girl,* like the white cupcakes?"

His face shut down again. "It was a celebration in absentia."

"Oh, I see." No, she didn't see at all. Someone was away? Gone? Dead? Was it a family member? Friend? Girlfriend or ex-girlfriend? Wife or ex-wife? She'd ask, but he was looking miserable again, and she wanted the sexy smiling guy back.

"What's your name?"

He brought his eyes back to hers. Somehow she managed

not to pass out. Or giggle. Or shriek and clutch her chest. God he was gorgeous.

"Sorry. I'm Daniel." He stepped forward and extended his hand across the case. "Daniel Flynn."

Daniel. Good name. She loved when people didn't shorten good names to one-syllable nicknames. Christopher. Benjamin. Alexander. And Daniel …

She took his hand, warm and strong with nice long fingers. Men's hands turned her on. And men's shoulders. And biceps. And butts. Chests were nice, too, and there was nothing wrong with strong thighs or decently shaped feet.

From where she was standing it looked as if Daniel might have it all.

"It's nice to see you again. I'm glad you liked the chocolate cupcake. Anything I can get for you today?"

A long, naked back rub?

"Oh." He glanced around the cases. "I wasn't really planning…"

"Greek pastry? Italian? French?"

His eyes wandered to her bread shelf. "Maybe a loaf of something."

"What's your favorite?"

"Oatmeal."

"Mine, too." She glanced quickly at the loaves. "I'm out here, but I have more in the back, can you wait a second?"

"Sure."

Angela started to turn, when an idea occurred to her. If she got the bread, came back and sold it to him, he'd have run out of reasons to be there. Which would give them maybe five more minutes to talk before he left her with no idea when or if she'd see him again. She needed more time to work around to asking if he was involved with anyone. Maybe not the greatest move—asking out a customer—but Daniel had finally woken her long-dormant interest in dating, and well…here he was. She didn't know any other guys she'd want to date.

Jack and Seth were both sexy, but Seth belonged with Bonnie, though he was too dense to figure it out, and Jack wasn't her type, nor she his. Besides, going after either of them would be like trying to date one of her brothers.

She turned back to find Daniel studying her curiously. Not surprising since she'd taken one step toward retrieving his bread and then had frozen as if she'd gone into a coma.

"Would you like to come back and see what goes on in a bakery kitchen?" She gave an awkward laugh. Oof. The invitation came out sounding even lamer than it was. A bakery kitchen? Like she was offering him a glimpse of the Holy Grail?

"Sure." He walked around the counter and joined her without hesitation.

Oh, my. Oh, gosh. He smelled really, really good, and given that she worked among some of the best smells in the world, that was really saying something. She wanted to touch him pretty much everywhere, but mostly she wanted to run her hands down his arms, shoulder to wrist, to see if they were as rock hard as they looked. Not since Tom had she had such a strong physical reaction to a man. And if that weren't a huge red flag right there, she didn't know what would be.

Except this time, she was just going to enjoy the attraction as the primal sexual response it was. This time she was not going to start dressing up simple lust with emotions it didn't deserve, not assign to basic animal reaction any happy-ever-after importance or expectations of True Love. Fool her once, shame on her, fool her twice, she was a total moron.

She led him into her kitchen, feeling a swell of pride, hoping he could see its beauty the way she did. Sacks of flour stacked two and three feet high. Bags of seeds, sugars, specialty flours and containers of nuts and dried fruits. Her fifty-kilo dough mixer, which Alice would be bent over later in the day; the gleaming metal work table where José shaped loaves; her triple-deck oven; tall metal cooling racks where Frank did the baking—all secondhand, but working perfectly.

"This is great." He stood in the center of the room, tall, vividly dressed, masculine, looking foreign. Angela had gotten so used to seeing everyone in flour-dusted aprons and jeans. "How does it all work?"

"I have a great staff." She counted on her fingers. "Alice mixes the doughs, José shapes them, Frank bakes and Scott comes here and there to do random cleaning and help man the counter when he's not in school."

He turned from perusing the bags of specialty flours. "And you slack off all day."

"I do. But when I'm not doing that, I develop new recipes, do most of the pastry baking, make up the schedule, balance the books, maintain inventory, try to get new accounts, put out fires…" She knocked wood. "Figuratively speaking."

"Is this what you always wanted to do?"

"I've always loved baking. But it wasn't until my honeymoon…" She practically choked on the words, then noticed his glance flicking to her left hand and realized what that sounded like. "I mean my ex-honeymoon. I mean my honeymoon with my *ex*."

Smooth, Angela.

"I'm sorry."

"Don't be. I've moved on." Though from the sound of her voice she was still bitter, a sound she needed to change if she were going to do this dating thing again.

"So you decided to be a baker during your honeymoon…"

"I was always a baker. Always had a dream of owning my own place. But in Europe I became really obsessed. I couldn't go to enough of the shops over there. When we got home, I got a job at a bakery and learned the business. When Jack came to the rest of us with the idea of buying a building together, I jumped at it."

"Jack? Rest of who?"

Angela made herself slow down. "Jack Shea has the photography studio down the hall. All the business owners at Come to Your Senses went to the U of Washington Seattle and graduated four years ago. We live in the apartments upstairs."

"Okay, I get it now." He ran his hand along the edge of her work table. Such great hands. "Must be nice to have friends around. Starting a business is tough."

"Yes, it's a huge plus." She gave a little laugh. "I guess that makes us friends with benefits."

This attempt at a joke fell as flat as her first croissant. Now he probably thought they were all sleeping together. So much for trying to let him know she was available. "How about you? What do you do? Oh, here, try this."

She handed him a piece of her chocolate-orange pistachio baklava, a new recipe she had high hopes for.

He bit, chewed. Both eyebrows went up. "Hmm. Nice. Thanks."

Nice? She wasn't after nice, she was after *wow*. But maybe he was shy about being effusive, or thought it wasn't manly. Tom had barely ever let a compliment pass his lips, as if he were afraid strengthening someone else would weaken him.

"Glad you like it."

"I work at Slatewood International."

Angela's ears perked up, even as she hated herself for letting Tom's words get to her. Slatewood was a huge manufacturing conglomerate headquartered in Seattle. She'd tried, admittedly lamely, to get noticed at some of the larger local companies but without luck. Maybe having an employee to get her in the door would help. Landing a corporate account would be a coup even Tom couldn't sneer at. "Really. Slatewood. Doing what?"

"Security specialist. Trying to keep one step ahead of scammers, hackers, phishers and so on."

"That's a big job."

He shrugged modestly. "I enjoy it. Kind of a good vs. evil battle."

"And you get to be the superhero. One of these?" She passed him one of her most popular cookies, based on the lowly oatmeal raisin, changed by supplementing the cinnamon with allspice and cardamom, and substituting dried currants and cranberries for raisins. Pretty basic, but good.

Another bite. More chewing. His jaw slowed. His eyes closed in bliss. "Oh, my God, that's amazing."

"Oh. Thank you." Angela plunked her hands on her hips, forcing herself to look pleased. So he wasn't afraid to compliment. Apparently for some tastes the baklava recipe wouldn't fly as is. She'd need to do more fiddling. "Would you like to take some home?"

"Absolutely."

"Just for you or is there someone…living with you?"

"I have a roommate."

A roommate. "How many do you think he—" deliberate pause "—or *she* can eat?"

"He can eat a lot."

He. She hid a grin as she packed a dozen cookies, freshly baked, into a box. "That'll last an hour or two. Those are on the house, by the way. You can always come back for more."

He took the box. "Thank you, Angela."

"You're welcome." They stood there for way too long, both holding the box, gazing at each other until it got really awkward and embarrassing.

"Um. My oatmeal bread."

"Right. Yes. Okay." She didn't move or look away. He didn't, either. He was so beautiful….

Oatmeal. Right. *Let go of the cookies, Angela.*

She made herself relinquish them, forced her eyes away from his. Headed for the wrong rack. Had to stop and change direction. Picked up a multigrain loaf. Had to put it down.

Picked up another. Oatmeal! Her brain had apparently re-booted.

She slid the fragrant fine-grained loaf into a paper bag, aware that she was ostensibly handing Daniel his walking papers. If she were going to suggest they get together again, she would have to do it now, and make it clearer than a general invitation to come back for more cookies. Otherwise she was going to stand behind the counter all day, every day, for the next who-knew-how-long hoping he'd come by again, which was pathetic.

Angela slid the bread on top of the box of cookies he was carrying, stood too close and looked up coyly. "Daniel. I was wondering…"

His eyes widened. He took a step back she could only hope was involuntary. Not a confidence builder. Had she only imagined the pull between them?

She let the sentence hang, nerves fraying. If he turned and left now, if he changed the subject, if he took another step back, she'd drop the idea entirely.

He didn't. He stood, somberly, waiting, apparently, for the ax to come down.

So be it.

"I don't usually do this. I mean I've never done this. It's not really my habit…I mean you're a customer and it's not really right for me to…that is, I was wondering if you'd like to get together sometime. Somewhere. For…something."

Oh. My. God. The all-time worst invitation that had ever been issued since the dawn of time. Why couldn't she be cool and collected, say something like, "Hey, wanna catch a movie sometime?" Or, "I hear the bartender at such-and-such makes a mean mojito, care to join me?"

No. She'd asked the most exciting man she'd met in years, if he'd like sometime, somewhere to do something.

Shakespeare, eat your heart out.

"Angela."

She was annoyed now. At herself, and perversely, illogically, at him. "That's me."

"I really can't."

Big surprise. "You're involved with someone."

"No."

"Gay?"

He looked appalled. *"No."*

"Not interested?"

"Definitely not that."

Oh, my. Her once-mighty irritation turned tail and ran. That was nice. Really very nice.

"Your mom won't let you?"

That incredible smile broke free again, accompanied by a deep laugh she could curl up in all night long.

"Nothing like that. The truth is…" He shuffled the bread and cookies, shifted his weight, then back. "The truth is, Angela, I promised someone a long time ago that I wouldn't date anyone. For a while."

She blinked. Blinked again. *What?* "How…long of a while?"

"It's been a year and a half so far."

She nearly choked. A year and a half! "And…this is supposed to go on how much longer?"

"Another six months."

Good God. *Two years* of celibacy? What kind of person would extract a promise like that? "Is this a possible priesthood thing?"

"No, no, it's not about religion."

She simply stared.

Daniel glanced impatiently at the ceiling and sighed. "I guess I better tell you the story."

"You don't have to." Of course he did; she was dying to hear. "It's not really any of my business."

But tell it anyway.

"I was engaged. She passed away. And I promised her..." He had the grace to look sheepish. "Okay, it sounds odd now."

Angela was pleading the Fifth on that one.

"But it was...she asked me not to date until our planned wedding date passed. Which is six months from now."

Good God. Angela's first try at dating and she'd managed to stumble over an unbelievably sexy, magnetically masculine, completely dysfunctional weirdo who'd engaged himself to a controlling, selfish horror of a person whose hold on him was even more diabolical than Tom's on her.

Though he was in one way, at least, the antithesis of Tom, who didn't let marriage vows even slow him down screwing the first woman he wanted. This guy had honored a vow that denied him a basic human need, a vow the woman he'd made it to wouldn't even know or be able to care if he broke. Zero repercussions except from his own guilt and damaged sense of honor.

She couldn't help admiring that quality. On some level this was a noble and romantic sacrifice for the woman he'd loved.

On the other hand...what a *colossal* waste. And what was this woman thinking when she extracted such a promise? That the sun rose and set on her and he needed to keep it that way even after she was gone? Angela tried to put herself in the same position and couldn't imagine saying to a man she loved anything but, "Go out there and be happy. Keep living your life as fully as you can. I am not and never should be your entire world." Maybe she'd be selfish enough to ask him not to forget her, but that was it.

It might not be polite to disrespect dead people, but Angela was pretty sure she wouldn't have liked this chick. Not as a friend for herself and not as a match for Daniel. White-on-white should not be paired with a chocolate guy.

"Well." She tried to speak brightly, but disappointment was deeper than she'd expected. "I guess that's a no, then."

"I'm sorry." He had a funny bewildered expression on his face, as if he were finding out he really was sorry, and it surprised him. Sorry and embarrassed and maybe a bit wistful.

His expression gave Angela permission to have a really wonderful and slightly devious idea.

She'd need to do this carefully and make sure she wasn't stepping over sacred boundaries, but what if she used the power of their attraction, which she was sure now she hadn't imagined, for a good purpose? Something more selfless than satisfying her hunger for touch and physical intimacy, which frankly Daniel had wrenched awake—a greedy, cranky, post-hibernation bear of a hunger. Something that would set him free from the unnecessary trap he found himself in, that would strike a blow for men and women everywhere who were unable to break free of ex-lovers, fiancés and spouses. Something that would make Daniel realize that he might owe this woman his past love and fond memories, but that he absolutely did not owe her from-the-grave dictatorship over his actions or his feelings or his body, and especially not over the pursuit of his own happiness, which was a constitutional right.

Something like Angela getting to know him. Becoming friends with him. And when he least expected having his unreasonable and unnecessary sentence commuted...

Seducing him.

5

SETH TOOK A long swig of beer, burped at a healthy volume and set the bottle back on the scratched, wobbly coffee table he and Jack had carried up from the street where someone had abandoned it. "We should do this more often."

"What, belch?" Angela sent Seth a disapproving look. Boys would, unfailingly, be boys.

"You're a pig, Seth," Bonnie said mildly.

"But I'm the best darn pig I can be." Seth gestured around the room. "I meant how we're here talking about something other than mortgages and business plans and profit margins."

"You're right." Jack helped himself to a handful of Cheetos Puffs. "This venture turned us into grown-ups too soon. We need to reclaim our inner frat boys."

"And girls," Bonnie said.

Seth held up his Elysian Fields Pale Ale in a toast. "I vote we do this once a month at least. For our sanity if nothing else."

"Hear, hear." Angela looked up from her busy job coveting Cheetos. Given how many baked goods she needed to sample, she tried to limit her snack intake. "That's actually an important point, Seth."

"Actually? Like I don't usually have important points?"

"Just on top of your head." Bonnie blew him a kiss.

"I meant that we've had some rough times and will probably keep having them." Angela held up her bottle, too. "Here's to continuing to keep our sanity. Which in the last year I'm convinced would have been long gone without you guys."

Jack hoisted his ale. "And then some."

The four of them were sitting in the living room of the building's vacant sixth apartment, which they'd agreed to use as a common area. Each of them had donated whatever leftover odds and ends of furniture and kitchen equipment they didn't need in their own places, and regularly contributed toward keeping the refrigerator and cabinets stocked with wine, beer and snack foods for times when they needed to meet, or, as Seth pointed out they did all too rarely, get together and unwind.

Tonight Bonnie and Seth shared the hideous olive-green couch they'd scored from Seth's parents' basement, each sitting rather pointedly, Angela thought, at either end. Jack sprawled in an overstuffed, worn rust-colored easy chair from Bonnie's grandmother, and Angela perched in the graceful wooden rocker she inherited from Aunt Dorcas, which hadn't fit anywhere else in her apartment. Demi Anderson, Caroline's friend, who'd taken over her massage therapy studio, and whom none of them knew well, had donated the black-and-white leather love seat that looked as if it belonged on the set of a futuristic movie. The four of them rarely sat on it. Silly, because it was in perfect condition and comfortable. Somehow they felt as if they were trespassing. Kind of how Demi seemed to feel around them.

"Jack, you haven't talked about your artsy-fartsy work recently, what's going on with that?" Bonnie changed position on the sofa to face Jack, which Angela couldn't help noticing brought her about three inches closer to Seth.

"I haven't talked about it because I haven't been doing any." Jack rolled his eyes, rubbing his hand across his cropped dark hair. He had perfected the art of the sexy scruffy look, and if he wasn't so funny and charming he could be the kind of guy whose bubble needed serious bursting. Angela couldn't wait until he met his match in a woman who'd have no trouble doing that when necessary. He and Bonnie had a brief fling before the quintet moved in together, and though it hadn't worked out, she was just the type of nononsense chick Angela thought Jack needed. "I spent the weekend coping with another nightmare wedding."

"Uh-oh. Bridezilla, part fifty-four?" Seth asked.

"Worse."

"Groomzilla?" Bonnie guessed.

"Bride's-parentzilla." Jack slugged down some beer and shuddered. "Not a single pose or expression was too ordinary for me to capture. It was all I could do to remind them there were other people there, too. Like the groom and his family. Oh, and they made the wedding couple replay the first bite of cake about five times because it wasn't 'cute' enough. Those kids are doomed."

"Of course they are." Seth snorted. "They're getting married."

"Stop. Now."

"Aw, c'mon." Seth gave Bonnie a friendly poke on the shoulder. "I have to say stuff like that. It's my job."

Bonnie rolled her green eyes and turned back to Jack. "I thought you had a new project lined up for the Unko Gallery."

"I have an idea. The owner is interested. I haven't been able to find the right model, though."

"What kind of series this time?" Angela was genuinely curious, but pretty sure she wouldn't care for the answer. No question Jack was a brilliant photographer, but his work always managed to make her uneasy, which she supposed was part of its brilliance. She was just one of those people who preferred that art filled her with joy rather than nameless dread.

"A commentary on the country's attitudes toward sex. How they sell it on every corner and label anyone who expresses interest as a degenerate."

Angela wasn't sure she wanted to know how he intended to depict that.

"What kind of model haven't you been able to find?"

"Girl-next-door. Totally virginal and innocent." His eyes came to rest on Bonnie's faintly freckled skin and auburn hair. "She'll have to wear a dominatrix outfit in one shot."

"Ooh, sign me up for that action." Bonnie winked at him.

"Really? You'd want to try it?" Jack looked her over carefully. "I'm not sure. I could do a test. You'd need to be okay naked in front of a camera."

"Huh." Seth jumped up and disappeared into the kitchen. Seconds later, they heard an empty bottle hitting the bottom of the recycling bin with unnecessary force.

Bonnie gazed after him, giggling. "Maybe I should take a pass."

"I was actually thinking you might like to do a similar shot with flowers. Maybe publicity for Bonnie Blooms? With that pretty face of yours, you'd be a great advertisement for your own store."

"Oh, you are such a sweetheart." She smiled adoringly at Jack. Seth emerged with another beer at his lips, trying to hide his scowl. "I'd love that."

"Want to try some out?"

"I'm all yours."

"I knew that about you." Jack sent her his signature smoldering look, a thing of beauty and power.

"You guys need a room?" Seth threw himself back down on the sofa, closer to Bonnie this time.

"Of course not," Bonnie said. "We can do it anywhere."

"Say please and I'll give you space right here." Seth patted the cushion between him and Bonnie, now partly occupied by each of them.

"By the way, Seth," Jack said. "Who was that total babe you had up in your room yesterday?"

Seth glanced at Bonnie, who was trying to pretend her expression hadn't just fallen about a mile. Angela groaned silently. Those two needed to get over it or get on with it.

"Oh, her." Seth waved the concept away. "She's a friend."

"Really." Jack winked at him. "How friendly does she get?"

"*Speaking* of hotties," Bonnie interrupted. "Angela, tell us about that bike-riding dude who came into your shop today for the second day in a row."

"The guy she couldn't take her eyes off of?" Seth's deliberately effeminate *do*-tell look, complete with wide eyes and prudishly puckered lips, cracked Angela up when she was trying very hard to glare.

"What makes you think I couldn't take my eyes off—"

"Bonnie was spying on you. She had high-powered binoculars and a wide range of sophisticated listening devices. Me, I just *happened* to be there. A *totally* innocent bystander who—oof." Seth caught a pillow, which Bonnie had hurled expertly, in the face. Like Angela, Bonnie had four brothers. Bonnie could take care of herself.

"I think we are waiting for *Angela* to speak now." Bonnie turned a true schoolmarm look of disapproval on Seth, who winked charmingly, then hurled the pillow right back at her.

Seth had brothers, too.

"Go on, Angela," Jack said.

"Not much to tell." Angela felt herself blushing. "His name is Daniel Flynn."

"And?" Bonnie prompted.

"He works at Slatewood International, writing security code."

"Ooh, good salary. He gets points for that. And a great ass. And adorable." Bonnie gestured to Angela. "More, more."

"He is single." She found herself hesitating, speaking

slowly. She felt as if her hopes around Daniel existed in a safe place in her thoughts, and if she pulled any out to share, she risked exposing them to ruin.

Strange, but true.

"And?" Bonnie was practically bouncing off the cushions. "Did he ask you out?"

"Not exactly." She took a deep breath, then allowed a small smile. "I asked him."

"Woo-hoo!" Bonnie jumped up for a high five, her short orange pleated skirt flaring. "You go, girl. When are you going out?"

"We almost weren't."

"What? Why not?" Bonnie backed up without taking her eyes off Angela. Seth put a hand to her thigh to guide her to sitting—even closer to him than before.

"Get this." Angela leaned the rocker forward and gave in to the siren call of Cheetos. One handful wouldn't kill her. "His former fiancée made him promise on her deathbed that he wouldn't date anyone for two years."

Bonnie's jaw dropped. "Oh, my God."

"Holy shit." Seth's nose wrinkled as if he'd smelled something foul. "That is just inhuman."

Jack winced. "Can she *do* that?"

"So…he's not dating?" Bonnie asked.

"He's not." Angela shrugged. "Unbelievable."

"That is weird." Bonnie frowned thoughtfully at her beer, while Seth and Jack contorted themselves in various ways meant to represent death from sexual deprivation. "But it's also really romantic."

"Be serious." Seth snapped out of impending rigor mortis.

"No, no, I am. I know, it was a lot to ask, and probably not fair. I just mean that he did promise and now he's honoring it." She looked suddenly stricken. "Wait, though, Angela, how much longer?"

Angela sighed. "Six months."

Bonnie sucked in a pained breath. "Ouch."

"Two years of celib— Celiba—" Jack pretended to be choking on the word.

"Ce-lib-a-cy," Bonnie said loudly. "Sitting home night after night with *Hustler* and the internet."

Jack cringed in on himself as if he were imploding. "Help…me…"

"You know what?" Seth shook his head firmly. "I'm not buying it."

"What, you think he's lying?" Bonnie asked.

"I bet you anything it's a line he uses on women to get them all schmoopy at how loyal he is and how noble, and then bang." Seth snapped his fingers. "He's got 'em. Piece of cake. The only hard part is getting anyone to believe such stup—"

Bonnie coughed extra loud.

Seth looked genuinely stricken. "Angela, I didn't mean…"

Angela shrugged. Weird as it might sound, she had believed him. No one could fake that kind of pain or vulnerability. And even if he did deserve an Oscar for his performance, she'd been planning to get what she wanted from him in a slightly twisted way herself, which didn't leave her much solid outrage to get behind. "I guess I'm as much of a sucker from Iowa as I look."

Bonnie bristled. "You don't know that he's lying. Not all guys are complete scum like those in this room."

"Yeah, okay." Seth held up his hands. "I just can't imagine any guy promising something like that."

"No, *you* can't," Bonnie said primly. "But that doesn't mean squat."

"Sorry, Angela, I'm with Seth on this one." Jack got up and headed for the kitchen. "Something weird about this guy. I'd be careful."

Angela sighed. What had she just been thinking about not sharing her hopes about Daniel for fear they'd be destroyed?

"Oh. Hi. Did I miss a meeting notice?" Demi stood uncertainly in the doorway, wearing black as usual—a scoop-necked clingy top and tight black pants that showed off her slender figure. On her arms hung silver bracelets, and the silver chain she invariably wore sparkled around her neck. She had medium-length straight dark hair parted slightly off to one side, and large exquisite eyes of an unusual gray color. The rest of her face was unremarkable except for an adorably dimpled chin. She was one of those women who exuded glamorous beauty no matter what because of her remarkable grace and style.

"Nope. We're just hanging out." Seth craned his neck around and gestured her in. "C'mon in and have a seat. Beer's in the fridge."

"Oh." She glanced around the room, frowning. "I was going to take a shower and catch up on some reading."

"Plans were made to be broken." Jack held out the bottle he'd just gotten from the refrigerator. "Take mine, I'll get another."

She locked eyes with him for a beat too long, which made Bonnie and Angela exchange glances. "Thanks. Really. But not tonight."

"Okay." Jack flicked the top off, still watching her. "Another time maybe."

"Sure." She took a step back, then turned and disappeared through the apartment's front door.

"Brrrrr." Jack hugged himself. "A certain chill every time she's in the room."

Bonnie's eyebrow lifted. "Except when she was looking at you, Jack."

"Ha." He dropped into his chair for a *GQ* pose, hand on his knee, head tilted sexily to one side. "Can you blame her? Seriously?"

The room erupted into groans and snorts of derision.

"What is her problem?" Bonnie asked. "I can't believe

Caroline stuck us with her when she moved. What was she thinking?"

"She was thinking she had to sell her business fast, and this woman was buying," Seth said.

"Aw, come on, Bonnie," Angela protested. "We barely know her."

"Whose fault is that?"

Angela shrugged. "Maybe she's really shy."

"Maybe she's really stuck up," Bonnie said.

"See, this is why I worry about you." Jack pointed to Angela with his beer. "You always look for the best in everyone, which makes you a target for creeps and liars if you're not careful."

"Like my ex, who was both?"

"I want to hear more about this Daniel guy," Bonnie said. "How did you leave it? Are you going out or not?"

"We are."

Jack snorted. "Whaddaya know, he managed to suspend his monastic vows, ju-u-ust this once."

"And the other forty times," Seth said.

Angela grinned slyly. "I told him I wasn't asking him out on a date necessarily, that I was hoping to get my bakery in to his company."

"Oh, ho! She's playing her own game. I like that." Seth laughed, a white-toothed guffaw that turned his fierce masculinity into endearing goofiness.

"Actually it is sort of true," Angela said. "I could do worse than cater for Slatewood."

"How did he react?" Bonnie asked.

"He said maybe we could get together sometime and brainstorm how to make that happen." Angela waggled her eyebrows suggestively.

"Woo-hoo!" Bonnie jumped off the couch again and did a victory dance. "This is fabulous."

"What, like over coffee or something?" Jack asked.

Angela's triumphant grin could not be held back any longer. "Dinner."

"Yes!" Bonnie pumped her fist. "You're in."

Seth and Jack exchanged glances. "This is not good."

"Aw guys, come on." Bonnie flopped back down on the middle cushion, just about sitting next to Seth.

"You watch." Seth shifted his position casually, turning toward Angela, now close enough to touch Bonnie's shoulder with his bent arm along the back of the couch. "He'll spend the whole meal acting like he can't believe what a great time he's having. He'll order cocktails, then wine and make sure you have plenty. At the end of the date, he'll suggest a nightcap. Then on your doorstep, an I-can't-help-myself kiss and 'Oh, my God, Angela, this is like nothing I've ever felt before,' while he's counting on you to be thinking, 'Oh, gosh, I'm so *special* to him, what we have is really *special*,' and bingo, he gets what he was after the whole time."

"God, you are disgusting." Bonnie shoved at him. "Don't listen to him, Angela. It's great news you're going. I'm proud of you for putting yourself out there."

"I guess. Even if things don't work out it's worth getting a shot at Slatewood. I really want to move the new line of pastries."

"Good for you." Jack grinned. "If you can't get laid, at least get hired."

"Seriously?" Bonnie smacked her forehead. "Seriously, Jack?"

Angela shook her head, laughing. "Are you guys this horrible with other women?"

"Of course not." Seth was grinning. "We're trying to *sleep* with *them*."

"What he said." Jack's smile came on full force, warming his eyes. Bonnie and Angela dissolved into giggles. Who could do anything else when Jack and Seth turned on the man-charm? Angela was sure they regularly dropped women in their tracks.

She also knew Jack was incredibly solid, one of the really good guys in spite of his tendency to strut, especially when he and Seth tried to outdo each other with the Cro-Magnon routine. But underneath he had a sensitive, vulnerable side he rarely showed anyone. She knew it was there. Bonnie, too. But Angela would guess few other women had glimpsed anything but his tough-man act.

Seth on the other hand…Seth was a really, really nice guy who needed to grow up and get a clue. Given that he was pushing twenty-seven, like the rest of them, Angela wasn't laying great odds that would happen.

She looked meaningfully at Bonnie, noticing again that she looked too thin, too strained. "The *best* part is that I'm really breaking away from the mess of getting over Tom. Now I can get out there and find someone who won't treat me like crap, who won't play mind games by toying with other women while taking me for granted."

"You go, girlfriend." Bonnie pumped her fist, Angela's message obviously having blown straight over her head. Jack, however, lifted an eyebrow. He got it.

"So when is this epic battle of the manipulators?" Seth asked.

"Thursday." She laughed at the thrill, and at the irony of Seth looking at her with admiration for something other than her scones, the chocolate-chip version that could reduce him to begging.

Even a few weeks ago, the idea of going after a guy, any guy, would have made her panic. Now she was not going after "any guy," she was going after one of the hottest she'd met in a long time, deliberately, and with as much anticipation as nerves. Had she blossomed this much in such a short time, or was there something particularly powerful about her attraction to Daniel? Maybe Tom's engagement had set her free in some way. Or maybe it was the safety represented by Daniel's vow of chastity, making it unlikely he and Angela would go far. Perfect situation for taking that first tentative step.

Angela had gone from the protection of her parents to the protection of dorm life, straight to Tom. Emerging battered and bruised from divorce, she'd worked up to starting her dream job, which, while not setting the town on fire, showed the possibility of solid success. So much of the past three years had felt like clawing her way through the pain, step by step, just trying to survive.

Survive she had. And now, for the first time, she felt as if she were no longer just happy to be back on her feet, but ready to run fast and faster, until she could take off and really start living.

6

"No, no, no." Angela took off her six thousandth outfit and looked despairingly into her closet. She was meeting Daniel downtown at Fischer Grill in an hour, and the stunning ensemble she'd assembled in her mind hadn't looked anything like stunning when she was actually wearing it. Nothing else suited her mood or the weather or her figure or the way she wanted Daniel to see her: as The Irresistible Seductress. But she couldn't *look* as if she were trying to be The Irresistible Seductress, she had to look as if she was The Networking Professional arriving for a business meeting.

Which meant, for one, she'd need to keep her tongue from hanging out when she saw him.

Rose-colored suit with low-cut black top discarded. Too conservative, and her broad shoulders meant she couldn't wear a suit jacket without feeling like a linebacker.

Floral sweater over camisole with full ankle-length skirt discarded—too sweet.

Little black dress that made her look fabulous—too formal.

Slender figure-hugging pants with tunic top—too casual. Miniskirt—too much leg. Long skirt—not enough. Pants—too masculine. Shorts—too seasonal. Linen—too uptight. Cotton—too girlish. Tight was too sexual, loose was too unappealing. This didn't go with that, that didn't go with the other.

She'd worked late at the bakery, helping Alice troubleshoot a new cranberry-lemon muffin recipe, and now…an apparel crisis. Forty more minutes. Still no makeup. Only vague plans about how she'd steer the evening.

Time…to…*panic!*

No, no, she didn't have time to panic.

Her eye fell on a purple flowered camisole she'd already tried paired with a short-sleeved close-fitting purple sweater. Great top, but wearing it over pants made her look like a flight attendant, and over a full skirt she looked like a Swiss Miss gone horribly wrong.

Maybe with a slimmer skirt?

Twenty minutes later, she was made up—not too much, not too little—wearing the outfit—not perfect, but the best yet—with her hair pinned up in a French twist she'd be able to release with the pull of a pin or two or three in a sexy flourish, letting her hair tumble down in a glorious mass about her shoulders. Or that was the plan anyway. On her legs, sheer black hose. On her feet, high black heels she hadn't been able to wear with Tom because he didn't like her being so close to his height.

She'd be late. No two ways about it. But if she found a parking place close to the restaurant, she wouldn't be rudely late, just coyly.

Half an hour later, she practically pushed someone's car out of a spot he was just leaving, wrenching her little Kia into the space the second his rear bumper cleared the car in front of him. *Yes.*

She turned off the motor, shot out of the car into air still chilly in mid-April, turned to slam the door and noticed white powder on the front seat. *Oh, no.* It looked like confectioner's sugar from the emergency load she'd hauled the previous day.

Which meant the rest of it must be clinging to her ass. Black skirt. Not good.

She twisted around, swiping back and forth at her butt, which of course she couldn't see, and which made her teeter on the heels and catch her shoulder painfully on the open car door.

Super.

At least the parking spot was decently close to the restaurant, which was a small miracle given the parking situation in the city. Otherwise she'd have to sprint for it, and risk arriving breathless and sweaty.

A deep breath, and she headed down Sixth Avenue in an elegant saunter, aware that Fischer Grill had solid glass all around, so that if Daniel were watching, he'd see her approach.

A quick glance showed a familiar, very masculine blond head outlined by the entrance, face turned in her direction. Her stomach somersaulted. It was Daniel. Had to be.

She drew herself up, made her saunter even more elegant, concentrated on looking wildly and confidently sensual.

Until her heel caught in a crack in the pavement and brought her down. And her pride. And her hair.

Ow. She'd landed hard on her right knee and hands, scraping all three on the rough cement. Her right stocking was shredded. Blood beaded around bits of dirt over the burning pink mess that had become her kneecap.

Super.

Even better? Here he came, loping down the sidewalk toward her, not blown away by her blatant sexuality, but concerned for his clumsy date who'd gone "boom" and skinned her knee like an eight-year-old.

"Angela. You okay?"

"I'm fine." She rubbed her palms together to brush off the dirt, wincing at the sandpaper effect on her raw skin. "Just a klutz."

"You came down hard. Let me see?"

She held out her hands on either side of her knee. "It's nothing. Really."

"Ouch. Those wide, shallow scrapes can be brutal. I fell off my bike last year, going fast. It was not fun." He took her elbow, helped her gently to her feet. "There's a drugstore down the street. Let's get that dirt off you before it causes trouble."

"Okay." She let him help her up, embarrassed to find her body shaking, typical overreaction to pain. If she ever got pregnant, she was asking for medication during the entire last month just in case.

A picture flashed into her mind of her in labor, Daniel holding her steady, as carefully and calmly as he was now. *There's a hospital down the street. Let's get that baby out of you before it causes trouble.*

She must be slightly hysterical.

"Thank you, Daniel." She laughed breathily, still having trouble calming down. "I'm sorry about this. It's not at all how I wanted to start our da—"

No, Angela. As far as he was concerned, this was not a date. Remember?

"Not a problem. Whoa, hold on." He pulled her back from the curb, which she'd just stepped off of without checking for cars, and nearly got run over by a speeding Prius.

Her heart sank. By now it was official: Project Seduction was a failure. In the back of her mind, Tom's voice again, accusing her of overreaching. *Why didn't she recognize her limits and be content with them?*

No. Tom was a self-serving prick whose main interest was in keeping Angela down so he could feel superior.

She straightened her shoulders to cross the street, forcing herself not to limp. The evening was only over when it was over.

In the store, she ditched her ruined pantyhose in the bathroom and grabbed a new pair from a nearby display. Then she and Daniel searched the shelves together and picked out a bottle of antibiotic spray, a small package of gauze and a box of extra-large adhesive bandages.

Being in the store with him felt strangely intimate, more than being together at the bar would have. Strangers belonged in bars. Buying everyday items in a drugstore was for established couples. It had been a long time since she'd enjoyed doing ordinary, everyday things with someone special.

Don't get used to it. Not with this one. Daniel was about getting her dating feet re-wetted, and about helping him escape the monastery his self-centered ex unreasonably imprisoned him in.

After he insisted on paying for supplies only she'd be using, Daniel led her to a bench on the street where he gestured her to sit.

She peered up at him with faux suspicion. "So we're going to play doctor now? Do I know you well enough for this game?"

His grin made her catch her breath. His blue eyes had caught the late evening light. His white teeth were surrounded by golden, smoothly shaved skin that looked as if it smelled and tasted wonderful. Angela sat, paralyzed, as if her body had stopped functioning. Certainly her brain had.

Daniel knelt at her feet; his fingers landed softly on her bare knee, shooting Angela through with arousal as if he'd touched her…somewhere else.

"I think we'll have to play doctor, Angela, even though we hardly know each other." His voice was low and slightly husky, his eyes didn't leave hers, so blue and so serious, humor dancing at their edges. "I promise I'll be gentle."

The drugstore plastic bag swished as he withdrew the spray, opened the nozzle. She watched his hands work, feeling breaths lodge in her throat, a solid mass.

"Palms first?"

She held them out. He took hold of her fingers and with a gauze pad wiped away the remaining dirt before he sprayed. The liquid was cool and comforting, soothing the sore heels of her hands, dripping between her fingers onto the sidewalk.

"Better?"

"Mmm." Her voice barely sounded. "Much."

The cool spray landed on her knee next, once, twice and again as he used the stream to dislodge black bits of Seattle's street. "Am I hurting you?"

"No." He could have been, she had no idea, felt nothing but the wild tension in her body, urging her to lean into him, touch his skin, feel his body's warmth.

Oh, my.

A trickle of antiseptic made its leisurely way down the top of her thigh. Daniel chased it with gauze, absorbed it with gentle pressure.

Angela swallowed audibly.

Wait, audibly? Weren't there street sounds? People around them? How could the city have quieted to the point where a swallow got air time?

She remembered the scene in the movie *West Side Story*, in which the hero and heroine met at a dance, and the frenzied crowd around them turned to a darkened, muted blur in the background, while Tony and Maria, vividly lit, had eyes only for each other, and the audience only for them.

The bandage emerged from its crackly paper wrapping, Daniel's large hands pressed it onto her knee, then lingered. "Okay now?"

She managed to meet his eyes.

"Yes," she croaked. "Thank you."

For another beat he stayed still, fingers warming her knee, eyes on hers. Then he reached for her.

Tonight, tonight, it all began tonight...

Angela held absolutely still, only breathing when she realized he was retrieving the pins that still clung to strands of her hair. One. Two. Three. He handed them to her.

"Thank you, Daniel. Again."

"You're welcome." His voice had risen to normal volume and steadiness; he stood abruptly. "Ready for dinner?"

"Yes." Angela shook herself into brisk reaction. *Boom,* it was over, regrettably, though she supposed they couldn't keep that intensity up all night, and too bad. "Absolutely. Dinner."

And a seriously stiff drink. And a happy reminder that all was clearly not lost. Her tumble seemed to have turned from disaster to gift. She and Daniel had established a connection; he'd been attentive and caring, and they'd gotten to play doctor....

All good things.

Inside the restaurant, after they were shown to their table, Angela excused herself to the restroom, where she put on the new pantyhose. Sheer black didn't look too hot stretched over a pink bandage, but it was better camouflage than nothing. She repinned her hair, smoothed it back and smiled. Her fall had been a slight glitch; now the rest of the evening would go on as planned.

Back at the table, she suggested martinis, only slightly ashamed of her intention to get Daniel tipsy so she could seduce him more easily. How would she feel if some guy got a friend of hers drunk with the intention of taking advantage?

Happily, she had a quick answer: if that friend was Bonnie and the guy was trying to set her free from Seth's hold on her, Angela would offer to pay for the drinks herself.

"So, tell me about your job at Slatewood." She folded her arms and leaned forward to expose her cleavage, gratified when his eyes flicked discreetly down to the display.

"I keep our data out of the hands of people who keep developing more and more different and sophisticated ways to get at it."

"A computer superhero, defending the innocent user from evil."

"More like a guy in an arcade playing Whack-A-Mole. You smack them down in one place, they pop up another."

"You enjoy it?"

"I get frustrated sometimes, always fighting people trying to do things I can't understand and don't respect, but from a technical standpoint, it's an always changing challenge and I do enjoy that, yes."

He appeared nervous, rubbing his hands on his thighs under the table, glancing around the restaurant. Maybe sitting across the table from a woman was feeling too date-like, and Angela should have suggested a bike ride or roller skating, or a walk, which would seem more platonic and therefore safer for him.

She willed the waitress to come with the drinks, so Daniel's inhibitions would relax, so she could work out a way to steer them back to the exciting intimacy and chemistry they'd had outside.

"How long have you been at Slatewood?"

"Two years. We moved out here from Chicago when Kate was due to start at U Washington's Foster School of Business."

"Oh, I see." Angela smiled overenthusiastically. Must avoid topic of Her Holiness at all costs. "Where did you grow up?"

"Highland Park. Outside Chicago."

"Chicago, right, you said." She nearly cheered when the waitress brought their drinks. If conversation was going to stay this dry all night, she'd need several. "Here's to you, Daniel. Thanks for helping me out by meeting me tonight."

"No problem." He hoisted his drink to meet hers and they both took a first sip.

"Mmm." She toasted him again. Took another, bigger swallow this time. "That is good."

He nodded, and gulped his third. Good. Time to get this party started.

"Tell me about the little boy Daniel. What was his life like?"

He narrowed his eyes. "Not a great childhood, but then not worth writing a dysfunctional-family novel about, either."

"No? Too bad. Those sell like crazy." She was pleased when he laughed.

"My parents were more interested in hating each other than raising a kid. I tried to stay out of their way. It was a pretty complicated time."

"I'm sorry." She laid her hand on his arm in sympathy, and left it there too long out of greed for the feel of his skin. "That must have been rough."

He shrugged. "I survived."

"Good choice."

He acknowledged the joke with a grin and sipped his drink again. "Tell me about your childhood. I'm sure it's a better story."

"I don't know about that. You ever see the movie *My Big Fat Greek Wedding*?"

"I did."

Angela raised her eyebrow meaningfully. "Then you've seen my family. Except mine wasn't so insistent on the Greek purity thing. Only Dad is Greek, Mom is apple-pie American."

"You look like her."

"How did you know?"

He leaned back, seeming more relaxed now, but whether it was the alcohol or the subject turning away from him, she didn't know. "You have an apple-pie face."

She winced. "Craggy and full of fat?"

When he stopped laughing, his face retained a hint of smile. His eyes had come alive again, and when he leaned forward, it was all she could do not to meet him halfway.

"Your skin is fair, not olive, your eyes are very light brown, your nose is small and straight. Your mouth…"

Angela held her breath. The way he was looking at it made her feel kissed already.

"I guess I have no idea what Greek mouths look like. But yours is…beautiful."

"Thank you." She barely managed a whisper. "So is yours."

And then they were back in that shimmering place of chemistry so powerful she could barely breathe. Had it ever been this intense with Tom? She couldn't remember. Right now it seemed as if she'd never felt anything like this for anyone in her life.

Stop, Angela. She was doing it again, assigning drama and substance to a simple chemical reaction. Her feelings were based on a normal human need for closeness, which was fine and healthy, as long as she recognized it for what it was. This time she wasn't going to plug the first guy she was hot for into the boyfriend slot, then close her eyes and keep going blindly forward. Plus, Daniel was still in love with his old girlfriend, and while Angela really wanted to help him break free of her claw-hold, she didn't want to be the first woman trying to fill those perfect shoes.

"So. I was telling you about my family."

Daniel jerked his gaze back up to hers. "Yes. Yes, your family. Go on."

"Okay." She had to desperately try to remember what she'd been telling him and where she left off. "Right, I was saying they're less intense Greekophiles than the family in the movie. My brothers and I dated whomever we chose, never mind nationality or religion. But it was pretty chaotic around our house. Lots of relatives, lots of noise, lots of good food. I'm sorry you didn't have that."

"I would have loved it." He was smiling again. "Especially the food. Is that what started you baking?"

"Oh, yes." She was immediately back in her mother's warm colorful kitchen in Cedar Rapids, Iowa, Grandma Loukas there, and Aunt Alena, coaxing sheets of phyllo dough into pans, chopping garlic, onion, squeezing lemons, roasting lamb. "I'd hang around the kitchen from the time I could walk, watching my mom and aunts and grandmother cook. As soon as I could hold a spoon they let me help. It was more a process of osmosis than teaching."

"You are very talented."

"Thank you." She beamed at him, thinking this was the perfect time to get her pitch for Slatewood over with, so she could concentrate on the seduction part of the evening. "You think the powers that be at Slatewood would be interested in hiring me? I have a new line of pastries I'm anxious to get going."

"They might be. There's a big company party every quarter. I can ask my boss about the Spring Fling. The problem is that his niece owns a French bakery here in town, and she's been in charge of dessert for years."

"Oh." Angela shouldn't be surprised. Same story all over Seattle. But it was still disappointing. Going after Slatewood might have been a way to trick Daniel into going out with her, but she'd love to get a foot in that door. "I can see the problem."

"I'll still ask. No harm in that."

"Thank you." She smiled, thinking of her peppery fruit tarts, the orange-pistachio baklava, lavender éclairs, and the recipe for rosemary-lemon Madeleines she was still trying to perfect. All unusual. All chic. "I'd be happy to come in anytime with samples and meet your boss or whoever's in charge. I'm probably cheaper than his niece if that carries any weight."

"It might." He put another dent in his martini and gestured to their menus. "Maybe we should decide on some food?"

"Good plan." She hid her grin behind the menu. Perfect.

She'd made her pitch, he hadn't seemed inclined to discuss it in great detail any more than she was, now they could order a nice bottle of wine with dinner and talk about other things. Like how terribly lonely he must be. How terribly lonely she was. How long it had been since she'd felt the touch of a man...

Oh, this would be good.

Except their dinner didn't come. And didn't come. The martinis were long-finished, and Angela's plot to get Daniel tipsy had backfired in that she hadn't planned to drink her entire drink, but now she had. And now *she* was tipsy, and getting hungrier by the second.

A short time later, an odd smell emanated from the kitchen. A smell like...

Smoke. Like something was...

Burning. Like...

The restaurant kitchen. And ...

Their dinners.

Seconds later, waiters were scattering through the dining room, sending out polite but urgent calls for the patrons to evacuate.

Daniel got to his feet and came around the table to help Angela to hers. "We better get out of here."

She didn't argue. Fire was not something to mess around with. "Darn it. I was looking forward to that salmon."

"Same here." He pushed through the door into the blessedly smoke-free chill of the street. "We'll have to find it somewhere else."

"Okay." She was hungry enough to be getting cranky. At this rate their nondate would go on all night and they still wouldn't have had dinner.

Yes, all night was what she'd had in mind, but not starving to death.

"I know the perfect place. It's not far. We can take my car."

They took his Honda over to Pike street and headed east.

The restaurant, an attractive bistro named Palms, wasn't far, but there was traffic and construction, and it ended up taking them nearly half an hour to get there, another fifteen to park and walk back to the entrance.

To find that it was closed for a private party.

Daniel stared at the sign on the door. "Am I under some kind of curse?"

Angela giggled. "I was starting to wonder the same about me."

"At this point I'm so hungry I don't care what we eat or where."

"Same here. Let's grab the nearest burger and inhale."

"Sam-Burger is near my house. It's close by."

Sam-Burger was close by, on E. Roy Street. And the line for tables stretched out the door.

"Desperate times call for desperate measures." Daniel put his hand to the small of her back and guided her past the waiting customers. "We can get take-out much faster, and eat at my place."

"I like your desperate measures." Had he really just invited her to his place? Perfect! Once again a seeming disaster had turned to her advantage. Restaurant fire leads to easy access to bed on first date.

Perfect.

Wait, she just said "perfect" already.

She really, really needed solid food in her system.

Daniel's apartment was around the corner on East 20th Avenue, a nondescript pale brick building. Angela walked in with him, trying to act nonchalant. Sure, she went home with men she didn't know all the time. No big deal, right? Women of the world like her...

And yet, she did feel safe with him. Maybe she was an idiot, but she trusted him. And she really loved walking up the stairs ahead of him, swaying her backside, which should be easy to notice if he cared to. When he stumbled, she even allowed herself to hope it was because the sight had knocked him stupid.

The hallway was underwhelming, beige and brown, stinky with new-carpet smell, and frankly, his apartment wasn't much cheerier though it smelled better. But she wasn't there for the decor, she was there for the *food* first and foremost, then the quiet intimacy being alone in his apartment would automatically provide. A nice long talk on his couch, maybe replaying Bonnie and Seth's constant scootching closer, until Angela made her move or invited Daniel's. She couldn't wait to experience that beautiful mouth of his. Everywhere.

Mmm.

He led her into the kitchen, pulled a couple of beers out of the refrigerator. Good beer, too, Mack & Jack's Serengeti Wheat. And a couple of plates. "Let's do this thing."

"I'm so ready." She and Daniel tore the wrappers off their burgers as if they were in a race, and sank their teeth in at the same instant. With that first bite, Angela got more than solid food in her system. She got a juicy, fresh, hot, beefy bit of heaven that practically made her moan with pleasure. Not to mention Daniel seemed to have relaxed a good deal once they crossed the threshold into his apartment. Why bringing a woman home would be less threatening than meeting her in public, Angela had no idea, unless he was lying about the girlfriend being dead. Or lying about her being an ex. Or lying that she even existed, the way Jack and Seth were so sure he was doing.

A tiny pang interfered with her burger arousal. She squashed it. If he was using her, that was all the better, because that's what she was doing, too.

"Good, huh?" He grinned at her over the top of his sesame-sprinkled bun and something lurched in her heart.

Oh, Angela.

"Really good. Whoever Sam is, I love him." She crammed

another bite into her mouth, too ravenous to bother being dainty.

"The owner's late father. French fry?" He offered her the paper packet and she indulged in several of the skinny, salty miracles.

"How do you keep your body so perfect with that place practically next door?"

"Well…" He tipped his head, looking amused but skeptical. "I didn't realize my body was perfect."

"Mmm-hmm." She swallowed a mouthful, nodding vigorously. "It is. Perfect."

"I take it you've given this some consideration."

"Serious consideration." She blinked at his chuckle. "What? I'm allowed."

"You are. And thank you." He gestured up and down. "You're…I mean you are—"

"No, no, don't even bother." She waved his words away. "No comparison. But thank you for trying to—"

"Let me finish." He leaned forward. "You are stunning, Angela. And if no one has made you feel that way recently, then you need to change who you've been hanging out with."

One fractional beat of intense silence, of desire palpable between them, then Angela's sharp, surprised breath sent a tiny piece of French fry into her lungs and reduced her to one of those fits of coughing that sound like either imminent death or throwing up. Neither of which were appropriate to the occasion.

Super.

"Angela." Daniel shot up and poured a quick glass of water, knelt next to her, gazing up at her red face, streaming eyes and convulsing body and offered it, tenderly rubbing her shoulder while she choked her way back into the ability to breathe normally. "You okay?"

"I'm not…" She gulped more water. "Not usually a disaster like this."

"That wasn't the word that came to mind."

"No?" She dabbed carefully at her eyes, hoping mascara and liner weren't pooling in black circles that would make her look like a plague victim on top of everything else. "You've been very sweet. I wouldn't blame you for thinking three or four times before going out with me a second time."

Daniel opened his mouth. No words came out. He stood up and went back to his seat.

Crap. She'd done it again. This wasn't a date. They were here to…

Oh, honestly. This was a date, and he had to know it. Pure semantics calling it anything else. Maybe it was time to make that clear.

"Daniel. I think we should talk about what kind of—"

An odd thumping in the front hall was followed by a rattling, then the crash of the apartment's front door flung open. More thumping, and rather animal vocalizations, only not the kind made by animals. The kind made by people who are screwing each other's brains out. Like animals.

The door slammed shut. The grunting, moaning and thumping continued.

Angela glanced across the table. Daniel looked as pale as she had been bright red a minute ago when she thought it was a good idea to try breathing French fry.

"Your roommate?" she whispered. A stunned nod from Daniel. "Ah. Well, he certainly sounds…healthy."

Daniel's glazed eyes turned to her and snapped into focus. Then a wonderful and really beautiful thing happened.

He laughed.

Not cautiously, not quietly, but with total abandon. Angela's heart responded again with that funny lurch, only more, and with a certain amount of triumph, too.

At the rich wonderful sound, the thumping and moaning stopped. Panicked whispers ensued. Scrambling. A door closed.

"Let's go." Daniel jumped to his feet and held out his hand. "Anywhere away from here."

"I'm so with you." She gave him her hand and got half-dragged, giggling, out of the kitchen. Opposite the closed door, Daniel paused.

"Hey, Jake. Just wanted to let you know we had a sudden need to take a nice lo-o-ong walk."

This time the front door slammed behind them, and they flew down to the stairs and into the street.

Four steps down the sidewalk, a sharp flash of lightning. Wind. Thunder.

There were never thunderstorms in Seattle. The temperature was too steady, too mild to build the requisite opposing forces needed for the explosions.

But there was apparently going to be one now.

"Angela."

"Yes, Daniel."

"I'm done fighting this curse. Would you like to walk in a violent storm with me and get completely soaked?"

"I thought you'd never ask."

He turned his face up, squinting at the black sky. "Fitting end to the evening, huh?"

"Couldn't be better. Or worse, depending on your view."

He still had her hand, and swung it as they walked down the street in the April rain, wind turning it even chillier. And somehow, instead of the next disaster on their date/nondate, the cold, drippy mess felt freeing and wonderful.

"I was thinking..." He squeezed her hand, sent her a sexy sidelong glance.

Angela's heart nearly stopped. "Yes?"

"That maybe we need a do-over on this evening, given that pretty much nothing has gone as planned."

"Oh." Somehow she managed to say the word calmly, which was a miracle, because she really wanted to be inappropriately childlike, shout, "Wheeee!" and run in circles. "I'd like that."

"Good." They crested a hill; Daniel stopped suddenly. "Look at that."

"What?" She peered down the steep incline, but nothing seemed out of place or odd.

"All that down…" He took a deep breath, a few steps, then a few more, increasing his pace, and then he was pulling her. "Run!"

She ran. Or maybe she flew, drops pelting her face, wind gusting, thunder crashing in the distance. Ran on and on, her energy seeming only to mount, her breathing barely taxed, so aware of Daniel beside her, his warm hand in hers and another evening promised to both of them.

At the bottom, they stopped, panting and laughing, giddy like fools. He turned, face alight, matching hers. His mouth stretched in a brief smile, then retracted.

"Angela…"

Boom.

Out of the sky a bolt of lightning so close the light was blinding, the metallic smell pungent, the accompanying crack of thunder nearly deafening. Angela shrieked, Daniel yelled, the rain started slamming. Then he was pulling her into the narrow shelter of a storefront, shielding her with his arms, turning them so his back was to the storm and she was protected, pressed against the shop door.

More giggles, more panting breaths.

"Oh, my gosh. That was terrifying."

"Really? You were scared? Not me, I was totally calm." He grinned when she lifted her head to give him a skeptical glare.

"I distinctly heard you yelp like a puppy." She hadn't realized how much taller he was until she was close like this. Really close.

"Yelp? Me?" His gaze focused intently, and Angela felt

her own smile fading, too. Her breath had been slowing, but now a new source of adrenaline sped it again. This moment between them was magic, standing toe-to-toe, water dripping from their skin and clothes, the rain now a constant steady drumming, the occasional car swishing past.

"Daniel." His name came out breathlessly. She had nothing to say, no thought of seduction anymore, she was caught in time with this man, whose name she simply had to say out loud, though she barely understood why.

He moved down, she moved up, and they were kissing. Not with the tentative exploration of a first kiss, not with the wild passion of lust, but with the practiced ease of a couple who already knew each other's mouths and tastes, the shape and pressure of each other's lips, the texture of hair under fingers, of muscle and skin under palms.

"Angela." Her name this time in the same helpless voice she'd used for his, as if he were also compelled by forces he didn't understand.

More kissing, lovely, lovely endless kissing that turned hotter and hotter the more it went on. Kissing that started taking over Angela's brain, until the arousal became so fierce she found herself clinging to his broad shoulders, pressing her pelvis against him, making please-please whimpering noises.

The kissing ended. He pulled back. Stepped away into the wet, looking confused and somber, wind ruffling his hair, his eyes a beautiful blue surprise against the clouds in his face.

Angela had gone too far, and seduction hadn't even been on her mind. She'd felt only a primal need to be closer, to feel his skin against hers, to keep kissing him, as much the seductee as the seductress.

"I'm sorry, Angela."

"I know, I understand. I'm sorry, too." No, she wasn't. Not at all. Not for a second was she sorry for anything that had happened between them since they met. But what had happened was too intense for the circumstances, and that was the last thing he needed. The last thing either of them needed. He was right. A little cool-down time was a good idea.

"I should go home."

He didn't object. Gave a slow nod and took her hand again. They walked in silence up the hill they'd run down with so much joy and abandon. He drove her back to Fischer Grill where they'd met, fire trucks gone, Closed sign in the window.

She pointed out her car, and got out into the rain, more of a sad drizzle now, the perfect accompaniment to her mood.

"Good night, Daniel." She managed a smile. "Thank you for the most unusual evening I've ever had."

He grinned then, that amazing smile that lit up his face. Angela got a lump in her throat—entirely too much feeling for the situation.

"I am not quite sure how, but I had a great time, Angela."

"I did, too."

She hovered for another second, hoping for a repeat of the do-over offer. A Mulligan for a poor shot on the first hole of their first course played together.

No offer. So she smiled again, closed his car door and walked to hers, knee hurting, hair a wet, tangled ruin around her face, shivering from the cold that hadn't bothered her a bit when Daniel had been beside her.

She wanted to see him again. More than she'd wanted anything in a long time. Maybe tomorrow she'd feel differently. Maybe she'd take a long look at her life and her feelings and decide a repeat date was the last thing she needed.

But right now with his taste still on her lips, with the sharp memory of his arms around her, his body pressed against hers—she wanted only one very simple thing:

More.

7

"Yo. HOPE YOU didn't strain anything getting here this early."
Daniel turned from his laptop, set up on the teak table in their
department's elegant conference room at Slatewood. Jake
was two hours late for work, arriving two minutes before a
meeting with their boss, Larry Kaiser, to discuss new cloud-
computing security strategies.

"Shut up." Jake slumped into the seat next to Daniel, pale
and bleary-eyed.

"She finally let you out of bed?"

"Yeah." He shook his head, smile pulling at his mouth.
"She's very…energetic."

"Uh, so we heard." Daniel closed an article he'd been reading online. "You seeing her again?"

"Nah." Jake powered up his laptop.

"Why not?"

"I don't think I'd survive another date." He grinned when
Daniel laughed. "*You're* in a good mood this morning. How
was *your* date?"

"It wasn't a date." Daniel was glad he didn't blush easily,
because the lie was a big one. Not a date. Yeah, that was why
he'd been a nervous wreck going to meet Angela and sitting
across from her at the restaurant. Why he'd panicked when

she fell, pushed bar patrons out of the way and run down the block to her side. Why he'd felt so protective wanting to get her cleaned and bandaged. And why when he touched that impossibly smooth skin of her thigh and felt her trembling, he'd wanted to make love to her on the bench right there on Sixth Avenue. He didn't even want to think about what he'd wanted to do to her while they were kissing.

And for that reason, he shouldn't see her again. Should put her entirely out of his mind. He'd promised a do-over after the disasters they'd had, but that was before he'd gone out of his mind and kissed her.

What was the right path? He didn't know. The vow to Kate had been so sacred for so long—up until the moment in Angela's bakery when Daniel had told her about the promise, saw her reaction and was then left with his own. Regret. Wistfulness. Annoyance.

For the first time the words he'd clung to, lived by for the last year and a half, felt uneasy. Over the top. Nearly ridiculous.

The feeling only got stronger when he'd spent a whole evening with Angela on their, uh, not-date. When he'd experienced her, hurt and trembling, sexy and fun, wet and breathless. Then in his arms, warm lips pressed to his, warm body pressed to—

God, he had to stop thinking like this.

"Oh, no, *not* a date, not at *all*." Jake jabbed in his password. "That's why you came home looking like you'd just seen Angelina Jolie naked."

"No comment."

"You going to see her again?"

He shifted. A little voice inside him was shouting, *Of course I'm going to see her.* But he wasn't about to open himself up to temptation. Temptation to break his promise before he'd thought the consequences through more carefully, and temptation for Jake to skewer him with teasing. "Nah."

Jake made a sound of disbelief. "Why not?"

"In your words, 'I don't think I'd survive another date.'" Or at least his vow to Kate wouldn't. Angela tested his resolve more than any other woman had. Not just the sexual attraction she held for him—he'd been attracted to a few women over the last year and a half. The danger lay in the fact that her personality was sexy to him, too. He loved the way she turned from wild to innocent and back. He lusted over the way she moved, with sensuality she seemed totally unaware of. And felt oddly tender watching her wolf down a burger, or braving a painful fall.

"You're not avoiding her because of Kate…." Jake waited for a response, then blew an impatient raspberry. "C'mon, Dan, this woman seems great."

"And you'd know this because you've spent so much time with her? What was she, a flash going past the door while you were banging some—"

"It's how you've been acting since you met her. Like you might have finally realized you didn't die along with your fiancée."

"I'm not acting any way." He snapped the words out, aware that right now he was acting like a kid busted in a big lie.

"Ah, okay. So I just imagined someone singing weird shit in the shower this morning?"

Busted again. He'd been singing up a storm—Frank Sinatra, the Beatles, Queen, Cage the Elephant.

"Total hallucination." He arranged his pad next to the laptop, put his pen horizontally across the top.

"Tawndee heard it, too."

"You'd believe someone named Tawndee?"

Jake snorted. "Point taken. But seriously, man. You seemed excited about this woman."

Jake had no idea. Thinking about kissing her, Daniel was practically getting hard right now under the conference table. Her ragged breathing and those hungry whimpers. He'd nearly—

"Good morning, gentlemen." Larry Kaiser burst into the room, bald head leading his peculiar gait, as if he were always about to take off and start flapping. "Sorry I'm late. You two are on time as usual."

"Yes, we are." Jake cleared his throat pointedly. "But we can always use a few extra minutes of preparation."

Daniel rolled his eyes. Suck-up.

"Anything going on?" Larry hoisted his case on the table and took out his laptop. "Just got in from the airport. Can't get a flight on time anywhere anymore."

"Nothing out of the ordinary, no," Jake said.

"All's good." Daniel looked down at his laptop, its edge parallel to the edge of the table, paper beside it, pen having rolled so it was no longer exactly horizontal. The urge to straighten it was ridiculously powerful. And it hit him, that besides being sexy, part of Angela's draw was her lack of right angles and straight lines, her shifting moods and energies. Kate had been all order and predictability, vital to him after the chaos of his upbringing. Angela...

Who was he kidding? He couldn't push her from his mind. Not even for ten minutes.

"Who's got what on the agenda?" Larry laid his Black-Berry on the table. "Or off the agenda?"

Off the agenda. Here was Daniel's opportunity to push Angela as he'd promised. "I was wondering about the Spring Fling this year."

"The party?" Larry looked up from his laptop in surprise. "What about it? You coming? Got a new date finally?"

"Ha!" Jake smirked. "As a matter of fact, he—"

"No, not that." He sent Jake a glare. Daniel hadn't been to any of the quarterly company parties since Kate died. "I stumbled over a potential caterer. Really talented. Just wondered if—"

"Caterer?" Larry's ears perked up. He was devoted to food in all forms, which his many hours in the gym couldn't erase from his middle. "What kind?"

"Bakery."

Larry booted up his machine, shaking his head. "No, no, out of the question. We have my niece, Nellie, for that."

"I know. She's incredible." She was. Angela couldn't compete in that arena. But… He took a deep breath, not sure if what he was about to do was the right thing. "This is different."

"Different how?"

"Less sophisticated. More regular stuff. Cookies, cupcakes." He called up the taste memory of those oatmeal cookies. "Sounds dull, but one bite and you realize how flat and tasteless the rest of your life—"

He broke off in horror. He'd been about to say "the rest of your life has been."

"Um, how the rest of your life eating cookies…has been… flat. And tasteless."

Silence as Jake and Larry looked at him in concern.

This was not good. "Her name is Angela Loukas. She owns A Taste for All Pleasures on Capitol Hill. She'd be happy to provide samples."

Angela would undoubtedly rather send pastry samples, but an in at Slatewood would be good for her business, and given Nell's talent, the cookies and cupcakes were her best chance. Her only chance.

Larry's left eyebrow raised. "Friend of yours?"

"Girlfriend of his."

"She's not—"

"Why didn't you say so?" Larry looked so pleased and was grinning so warmly that Daniel shut up. "Good for you. It's about time. Sure, bring in some samples, we'll see how she does. Now…"

He pulled up a file and the meeting was officially on.

Which meant it was an hour before Daniel could get Jake alone in their shared office and attempt to kill him.

"My *girlfriend?* Larry will tell Lucy and she'll tell everyone."

"So? It got Angela a chance." Jake smacked Daniel's chest with the back of his hand. "Lighten up. Wait until after he tries her stuff. If he's not into her, problem solved. If he wants to hire her, say you just broke up."

"Oh, for—"

"Angela isn't going to know." He backed toward his desk with a meaningful look. "And guess what, neither is Kate."

"Would you stop bringing up Kate like that?"

"Hmm." Jake looked thoughtful, then shook his head. "I doubt it."

Daniel sighed and dumped his laptop back on his desk. He should be seriously annoyed at his friend. Much more than he was. But it had just occurred to him that he now had a legitimate, nondate reason to talk to Angela again. To tell her that Larry would take a look at her cookies. Daniel would decide in the meantime whether another date could or should happen.

Though he had a feeling he already knew the answer.

"OH, MY NIGHTMARE, oh, my nightmare, oh, my ni-i-ightmare Madeleines." Angela thumped down a plate of the small shell-shaped French cakes on the coffee table in the group's shared apartment. "Hey, are we the only two who showed up for cleaning duty again?"

"Jack's coming. Seth has a lesson. Demi…" Bonnie rolled her eyes and poured scouring powder into the sink. "Who knows. Cookies still not cooperating?"

"Spongy. Crumb not delicate enough. I'm liking the rosemary-lemon flavor, though."

"Let me try. I bet they're fine." She peeled off her manicure-saving yellow rubber gloves, which clashed spectacularly with her sheer violet top, and made a beeline for the plate, grabbed a Madeleine and took a bite. Chewed thoughtfully. "Oh, how *spongy,* and what an *indelicate* crumb."

Angela snorted. "Uh-huh."

"I'm not wild about the rosemary in there, but the texture doesn't bother me." She finished the cookie and took another. "You're too picky."

"If I'm going to compete…"

"I know, I know, you want the glamor-bakery. Well, keep trying. You'll get it. I'm sure the five hundred and seventy-seventh recipe will be better."

"Only three hundred forty-five to go." Angela made a face. "I'll go get the cleaning stuff."

She went into the back room, a bedroom whose closet the group had taken over for supplies, and pulled out spray cleaner and a sponge, absently tossing her bakery apron on the bed. The group picked one Sunday evening a month to get together and clean the common room, since doing it on a rotating basis hadn't worked out. Someone was always busy on his or her day.

"So…" Back in the kitchen, Bonnie was still going at the sink, again wearing the horrible gloves. "I have not yet gotten the detailed report on The Man Who Cannot Date."

"I came by your place last night and you'd gone out."

"Oh. Yeah." Bonnie's voice turned ultracasual. "Seth and I went out for a drink."

Angela sighed. She didn't know whether to strangle Seth, Bonnie or both. Why did Bonnie keep doing this to herself? Could denial run that deep or was she simply a masochist? "Fun time?"

"Sure. He's always fun. So did you get Daniel to change his mind?"

"I don't know." Angela found herself scrubbing the same spot over and over, a spot that hadn't been that dirty in the first place. "I just…don't know."

"Well, that's not too helpful. What happened?"

"Pretty much everything went wrong. At the same time, it all managed to go right. I think." She pushed back a lock of hair that had escaped her ponytail. "I still don't know what I'm going to—"

"Excuse me." Bonnie held up a rubbery yellow hand. "Details first. Analysis later."

Angela told her the story of the multiple-disaster evening, laughing at how horrible it all sounded, but not able to quell the deep longing she'd been feeling every day since Thursday, whenever she thought of that time with Daniel. Longing for what exactly? Certainly for another chance to see him, another chance to seduce him. But Angela wished she could say the longing stopped there, where it was supposed to.

Granted, Daniel was the first guy she'd pushed past her fear to go out with, so she was undoubtedly giving him more importance than he deserved, and probably clinging too tightly to hope that something would come from it, even knowing dating could be a long bumpy road and it was seriously unlikely she'd land smoothly on her first try.

At the same time, while their kisses had been unbearably full of desire and passion, there had also been moments of pure sweetness, and tenderness so deep it bordered on pain.

Which was the best reason to want more, and the best reason to stay away.

"Uh, Angela?" Bonnie's voice was full of laughter. "I'm pretty sure that spot is clean."

"Oh." She looked down guiltily. Again, she'd picked out one place on the counter to rid of every possible germ, bacteria, speck of dust and probably the top layer of tile.

"I take it we're a little distracted."

"A little."

"He sounds fabulous, Angela." Bonnie patted her heart, gloves making a wet spot on her blouse. "I totally think you're on the—"

"Hey, sorry I'm late, what should I do?" Jack strode into the room, looking incredibly hot, as usual, in jeans and a white Panic at the Disco T-shirt.

"Fridge." Bonnie tossed him a sponge. "There's scary stuff in there. Late person gets that pleasure."

"Oh, goody." He squeezed Angela's shoulder as he went past. "Hey, babe, haven't seen you in a few days."

"Ms. Angela had her date on Thursday," Bonnie announced.

"Hey, that's right." Jack turned back and looked at her measuringly, dark hair rumpled in an endearing imitation of bedhead. "How was it?"

"Got time?"

He opened the refrigerator door and shuddered. "As long as this horror takes."

Angela recounted the story while Jack dove in to the job, quiet except for a few exclamations of disgust that escaped him when he opened a particularly noxious container.

"Wait." Jack turned questioningly. "*He* stopped the kissing?"

Angela nodded. She'd once seen a cyclist hit by a suddenly opened car door, and would never forget the look on his face: fear, pain and what-the-hell-just-happened astonishment. When Daniel pulled away in the drippy shop doorway, she'd undoubtedly been wearing the same stunned expression.

"Hmm." Jack gave a thoughtful nod. "Then he might be telling the truth about holding back and why. If he'd been trying to get laid, he would have kept at you."

"See?" Bonnie snapped off her gloves. "*Some* men are actually good people."

"Uh-huh. And not speaking of which—" Jack wiped down a section of the refrigerator shelf "—where did you and Seth go off to last night?"

The forced cheer was back on Bonnie's face. "Oh, we went out. Had a few drinks."

"You were back late." He recoiled from something spilled and held up his fingers. "Paper towel here? Maybe two?"

"What, do I have a curfew?" Bonnie threw him the whole roll.

"No." Jack tore off a towel and wiped his hands. "I'm watching out for you."

"I don't need—"

"Hey." Angela put her hand on Bonnie's shoulder, which felt startlingly thin. "I've been worrying about you, too. Seth is a terrific guy. A really terrific guy. But you deserve someone so much more—"

"I know, I *know*." Her voice rose with her emotion and she made a visible effort to relax. "Believe me, I know. You don't have to tell me. Nothing is going on, and nothing is going to go on. I'm over that, not going back."

Jack exchanged glances with Angela. "So what's been going on with the woman he's been hanging around with—Alexandra?"

Bonnie shrugged as if she couldn't care less, which neither of them believed. "He says nothing."

"You don't believe him," Angela said.

Bonnie stayed still. "I…don't know."

"Don't you see, Bonnie?" Angela tried to keep her voice calm. "You can't even trust him to tell you the truth."

"I know. I know, I know, I know, I *know*." She hurled the gloves down on the counter. "It sucks, I suck."

"If you want to fight dirty…" Jack sniffed cautiously at a carton of milk, and put it back into the refrigerator in obvious relief. "We could use my idea."

"I always want to fight dirty." Bonnie jammed her hands on her hips, close to tears. "What's your idea?"

"The picture I want to take of you, wearing only flowers.

It probably won't change anything but it would sure piss him off."

"No, no. That's not the way to handle this. You have power in other ways, Bonnie." Angela tried to keep the frustration out of her voice. "You're hot, you're beautiful, you're fun as hell. Men will be clawing at each other to get to you."

"Yeah, the line outside every day is overwhelming."

"You haven't tried." Angela glanced at Jack for support, but he was shaking his head. "Get out there and date someone else. I'm doing it."

"Uh. You went out once with a guy you're trying to trick into sleeping with you. How is that worse than leaving a photograph around?"

Angela's mouth opened for a retort, which didn't come. Seducing Daniel was the plan. That hadn't changed. So why did she feel as if she had to contradict Bonnie? "It's different."

"Tell me." Bonnie confronted Angela gravely. "If you thought dangling a picture of you mostly naked in front of Daniel would help your seduction effort, would you do it?"

Angela laughed. She didn't even have to think about that one. Of course not. She didn't need to play games like that, would never dangle herself naked to get a man jealous or coming after her. She'd just…

An image came to mind, of Daniel looking at a picture of her, naked except for carefully placed petals that didn't conceal much. His eyes were dark with lust, his pants bulged, his breathing was high and fast. She imagined him wanting her with such force that he threw down the picture and jumped into his car to get to her faster than his bike would take him. That he'd fling open the door to the bakery, turn her Open sign to Closed, vault over the counter and drag her into the back room.

"Well?" Bonnie demanded. "Wouldn't you do it?"

"No, but—" To her horror her voice thickened. "Daniel isn't. I'm not— He's…"

She gave up.

Bonnie's jaw dropped. "Oh, my God. You're falling for him."

"Uh-oh." Jack wasn't talking about something in the refrigerator that time.

"Ha!" Angela's shout came out in a froggy croak. "That's ridiculous. We had *one* date."

"That's all it takes. Jack, do we need an intervention here?"

"Hmm, don't think so. Except on this cheese." He tossed a moldy brick into the trash. "Is he falling for you? Sounds to me like he might be."

Angela desperately pushed the thought away. "We're not talking about me. We're talking about Bonnie. And Seth. I don't want him to be able to hurt her anymore."

"I don't want this guy to hurt you, either." Bonnie looked into Angela's eyes, her green gaze compelling. "Can he?"

Yes.

Immediately Angela started to panic. No. This was crazy. After one date? Daniel couldn't mean anything more to her than a reawakening of her desire to be part of a couple again. The danger was in romanticizing their encounter, romanticizing the fact that he was sweet to her and had kissed her. Tom had been sweet, he'd kissed her, Angela had labeled it love, and look how wrong she was then? Love took time. Love took intense work and a thorough understanding of each person's needs and how they interacted.

"I'm waiting…" Bonnie tapped her foot impatiently, but her eyes held only concern.

Angela threw up her hands. "I'm not—"

"Hi, sorry I'm late. I had an appointment go overtime." Demi came into the room, stopping when Angela and Bonnie both turned to stare blankly.

Her face fell. "Should I come back later?"

"No, no, not at all." Angela smiled warmly. "We're just discussing man trouble."

"Ah." She nodded a few times, looking back and forth between Bonnie, Jack and Angela. "Anything I can do?"

"Probably not." Bonnie spoke briskly. "Unless you can figure out a way to turn them into women."

"Don't think I can do that. I'll vacuum, though." She marched to the closet, took out the vacuum and disappeared into one of the back bedrooms.

Bonnie shook her head. "So sweet of her to be concerned."

"Now now," Angela said. "She probably thought it wasn't her business."

"Yeah, I guess it's not." She reached into the refrigerator over Jack's head and pulled out a Diet Coke. From the back bedroom the roar of the vacuum started. "You still haven't answered my question, Angela."

"What question was that, Bonnie?" She didn't want to answer any more questions about Daniel. She didn't even want to think about him anymore. Thinking about him only led to confusion and uncertainty, and given that Angela was only just emerging from three years of that, she wasn't anxious to return.

The vacuum noise stopped. Demi appeared in the sudden peace, holding out a cell phone with a familiar ring tone. "Angela, you left your cell in the back room in your apron. Looks like it's someone named Daniel."

DANIEL TOSSED his cell onto his bed. He'd call Angela later. Right now was not a good time, because…

Because…

Sighing, he resolutely picked up the cell again. Yesterday hadn't been a good time, either. Or the day before.

He'd say he was calling to discuss the catering situation at Slatewood, which was true. Or mostly true. No other subject needed to come up if it didn't seem right. Though he didn't feel so much that he was betraying Kate by calling. He just felt…

Really nervous.

For God's sake, had he become that much of a wimp that he couldn't call an attractive woman to discuss business? He had no problem talking firewalls and anti-virus programs, phishing and password strength with the few desirable women he encountered in his job.

But Angela wasn't just another desirable woman. She'd turned on in Daniel a nearly obsessive fascination that hadn't been activated since he'd met Kate back in his sophomore year of high school. He'd been standing outside a gas-station food store, smoking the cigarettes he didn't enjoy that much, working up the nerve to go inside and steal something to eat. He could still remember the chill of the Chicago air, the pungent smell of gasoline, the way everyone had seemed to be staring suspiciously. He had plenty of money in his wallet, but the guys he hung with all smoked and stole, and he'd been in a frenzy to prove to them and his parents that he was someone to be reckoned with.

Sounded pathetic now, but it had made perfect sense to his hurting, angry young self. He'd been about to go inside the store when a girl had come along. A woman, really, even at sixteen. Blond, with the straight, practical bob she'd wear her whole life, wearing jeans topped by a hot pink sweater that brought out the color in her cheeks and set off her blue eyes.

Daniel had felt immediately awkward and guilty, even though he hadn't done anything yet.

She'd stopped, frowning at him, jammed her hands on her hips. "You think smoking makes you look cool, but it doesn't. It's stupid."

He'd sneered at her, shame burning his cheeks a brighter color than her sweater.

"You'd be cuter without it." She'd tilted her head, eyeing

him appraisingly, then nodded as if she'd figured out everything about him and probably the universe as well. "Much cuter."

Daniel had been stunned. Cute? Him? The Invisible Kid? He'd really looked into her eyes then, and boom, in a hit-by-Cupid's-arrow moment, he'd fallen for her the way only sixteen-year-old naiveté makes possible.

"I'm Kate. I go to Highland Park High, too." She'd held out her hand for a shake. He'd been paralyzed by indecision, as conscious of his tough-guy image as he was of the strong desire to feel her skin against his palm.

"Fine. Whatever." She'd swept past him into the store, muttered, "Jerk." Daniel had been so flustered his cigarette, the last he'd ever smoked, had fallen out of his mouth and left a burn mark on his shoelace.

The encounter with Kate had been all his shaky confidence needed to turn tail and flee the potential crime scene.

The next day Daniel had looked for her at school, found her—of course she'd wanted him to—apologized, and clamped onto her like a lifeline. After that he'd spent more time at her house—ordered, neat, full of homemade cookies, family game nights and more laughter than he'd ever heard—than at his cold chaotic one, filled with angry silences, frozen dinners, stomping feet and hurled insults.

Daniel wasn't looking for rescue from his life now. If Kate hadn't found him, he might have self-destructed. Without Angela he'd still be himself. Just…lonely again.

He dialed the number for A Taste for All Pleasures—the phone rang, clicked, then rang again, as if the call had been forwarded. To her cell?

Another ring. Another. He was nearly ready to give up, when she answered.

"Hi. Daniel. Hi." She sounded breathless and surprised and pleased and unbelievably sexy.

"Hi, Angela." He turned in his bedroom and got a glimpse

of himself in the mirror over his dresser, grinning like an idiot. For crying out loud. "How are you? How's your knee?"

"Fine. Really fine. I've managed to stay upright and nothing has burst into flames around me. It *is* raining again, though."

"It's Seattle. Rain happens."

"Sometimes that can be nice." Her tone changed, bringing to mind what had gone on between them during the storm Thursday night. A quick sigh came over the line and he hoped she was thinking the same thing.

But this was a business call. "I spoke to my boss about you on Friday."

"Oh?" She was cautiously hopeful. He found himself hating to disappoint her, flashing back to Kate, who when he'd failed on some mission, anything from asking for a raise to buying a certain kind of bread, had acted as if she were disappointed to discover he was human. He wasn't sure how Angela would react.

"I mentioned your international pastries."

"Ye-e-s?"

He rubbed his forehead. This was not easy. "I have to be honest. He wasn't enthusiastic. His niece has a French bakery that—"

"Oh, right. You warned me. What place is hers?"

Her nonchalance surprised him. "Nell's on Fourth Avenue."

"Oh, yes, I've heard of it. I'll have to go check her out, see what she's doing."

"Yes. Sure. Good." He frowned in confusion, having braced himself to offer sympathy and apology to a woman who didn't seem to need either.

"So what was your sense, is all hope lost?" She didn't sound cheerful, but certainly not despondent. Daniel didn't get the slightest sense that she was about to demand he try again, or pitch a fit at what she'd perceived as his failure.

Most of the time Daniel respected the perfectionism that drove Kate, but on those occasions he'd learned it was best to roll his eyes and wait for her to calm down.

"Hope is not lost—Larry does want samples, as long as they don't duplicate Nell's contribution. Maybe you could send some of those cookies that—"

"No, no, not cookies. That's not the direction I want to expand in."

Again, he was taken aback. No? Kate would have done anything, pushed any button, pulled any string to get what she wanted, even part of what she wanted. She'd been a force of nature.

"You might want to reconsider. A foot in the door at Slatewood couldn't hurt. And those cookies I tasted were—"

"No. Thanks." She spoke firmly. "He wants samples, I'll send pastries. I think mine are unusual enough to stand on their own. If he doesn't like them, okay, we tried. Thank you for doing this for me, Daniel. It was really nice of you."

"You're welcome." He shrugged, picked up a shirt that had fallen from the bed onto the floor and balled it up. "We'll work out a time to hand over the samples, then."

"What are you doing right now?"

He froze with his arm back, ready to throw the shirt into his hamper across the room. Had he imagined the suggestive tone of her words? He pictured her, lovely shining eyes, beautiful curving mouth that tasted so sweet, smooth skin enveloping her hourglass body.

Temptation. Not for the first time. But this time it wasn't only Angela's sexual pull tempting him to reexamine his promise to Kate. It was Kate herself, and his relationship with her. It was the comments Jake had been making, which Daniel had rejected for the past eighteen months without really listening to. It was how odd and twisted the promise had sounded when he'd told Angela about it.

Kate hadn't been out to make his life hell after her death.

The vow had been asked for and given in a moment of shared agony over having to say goodbye to love they'd been sure would last forever. The promise was part of the denial stage of grief, a way of holding on to each other and to that love a little longer.

Maybe understanding the vow and what it really meant, or more importantly, what it didn't mean, could make it possible for him to move forward with Angela. Rather than betraying Kate, maybe Daniel was finally emerging from his grief, and grappling with a clearer picture of his life and his choices.

"Er…hello?" Angela's voice was cautious now. "I'm sorry, was this not a good time to suggest we—"

"No. No, it's fine." He launched the shirt, watched it sink into the hamper for a two-pointer, heart strangely full and oddly weighted. So much emotion, so much confusion over a simple visit to a bakery. But one thing remained clear in the shifting landscape of his emotions. Daniel wanted to see Angela again and he wanted to stop feeling miserable and dead to the world. "Believe it or not, Angela, this is the absolutely perfect time."

8

ANGELA HOVERED AT her bakery counter, jittery and excited. Daniel was on his way through Seattle's streets on another cloudy, chilly day, up and down its hills to A Taste for All Pleasures. That in itself was not surprising. She'd invited him after all. What had made her breath stutter and her skin warm was the way he'd responded. For the first time his voice had sounded alive, careless, his words had come out with passion and spontaneity.

Believe it or not, Angela, this is the absolutely perfect time.

Not words of transparent passion, but he'd said them as if they were.

Yes, she'd had a small setback when she'd caught herself imagining more between Daniel and her than simple attraction. But Angela had spent a good long time getting her head back on straight, talking herself out of that mistake, and had succeeded perfectly. It could well be that she was on her way to developing feelings for Daniel. It could well be that she had met the love of her life and they'd live happily ever after. Or it could be nothing even close to that.

The concept she was determined to keep front and center was that she didn't have enough information yet to know whether he was or wasn't, so there was no point even thinking about it. Her original plan was back on track, to free a fellow prisoner of a previous relationship. It was up to Daniel how seriously he took the promise to Control Freak Fiancée and whether he'd welcome that freedom or not.

Either way they would each take charge of what they wanted and needed right now, because right now was all they had to work with.

Her door opened, triggering a new song Seth had put in for her, Jason Mraz's "I'm Yours," and guess who walked into her shop. Her heart started sprinting. *Daniel.*

Except he looked different. She couldn't tell how. Still tall. Still handsome. Still built like a Greek statue. But…more somehow. More alive, more masculine. More himself.

She started getting ridiculously nervous.

He sauntered over to the counter. "Good evening, Ms. Loukas. The bakery is still open?"

"Only for you, Mr. Flynn. May I help you?"

"Yes." A slow grin. "I believe you can."

Oh, my. She was ready to hyperventilate. All she had to do was keep reminding herself *she* was in control, of the situation and of herself.

"You need pastry samples." She grabbed a flat cardboard box and crossed to the display case on her left, while Daniel kept pace on the other side of the counter. She could see his strong thighs through the glass, knew the shape and size of his butt, found herself picturing the muscles of both working on top of her, and nearly dropped the cardboard she was trying to unflatten into a box. *Steady, Angela.*

She grabbed her tongs and gathered her wits to start her selection. French first, a thyme-and-orange macaroon and a strawberry-balsamic millefeuille, a black-pepper *tarte aux fruits.* Then to some Italian specialities: an anisette cookie with passion fruit seeds and pignoli with sage. From Germany, tiny allspice vanilla linzer cookies alongside a slice of the cream-filled yeast cake, Bienenstich—her version with

Mexican chocolate. After a few other choices the box was full, looked and smelled wonderful. She'd count that as a good thing. "That ought to do it."

He took the package from her. "I'll make sure he gets this tomorrow morning."

"Thank you. Anything with cream should be refrigerated tonight."

"I'll remember." He glanced around the shop, then back at her with such sudden intensity she had to fight not to step back. Wait, this was supposed to be *her* seduction of *him*.

She was ready. Daniel didn't know yet, but no one was in the kitchen. Her bakery was closed on Mondays so the crew hadn't come in tonight. It was just him and her and lots of room and time to play.

"Daniel, would you like to come in the back with me? I have a new cookie for you to try."

"I'll try anything you make." He followed her into the space where the smell of last night's bread lingered, mixing with the aromas of the sweeter cakes and just-baked cookies she was experimenting with, her favorite smells all jumbled together.

Now add Daniel and she was nearly in heaven.

Nearly. That part she hoped would come next.

"I'll be right back." Angela sauntered out into the bakery, then dashed to turn her sign to Closed, turn out the shop lights and lock the door, making as little noise as possible, so he wouldn't know what she was doing, then dashed back toward the kitchen, putting on the brakes at the entrance so she could resume the sauntering thing when she was in view again.

She picked up a chocolate pistachio cranberry cookie, a recipe she'd only just perfected, having tried too many flawed versions with dried cherries before deciding cranberries gave the cookies a better balance of flavors. She broke off a bite and handed it to Daniel. "Try this."

"Ohhh." His groan was pure ecstasy, and got her shivery with anticipation. She wanted to hear him groan like that in a very different context.

"You like that?"

He nodded blissfully. "I *so* like that."

"Good." She took a step toward him, broke off another tiny piece of cookie that she ate herself, as sensually as possible. "You know, the best part of being a baker..." She took another step, ending about two inches from his broad chest, broke off another chunk and held it to Daniel's lips. He stood frozen for a beat, then opened them and took the piece in, not taking his eyes off hers. "...is giving people pleasure."

"Angela." Her name came out on a hoarse whisper.

She swayed forward. Her breasts grazed his chest. He inhaled sharply. Swallowed. His hands found her shoulders and he gripped them, staring down at her with tortured desire etched on his face, blue eyes dark with suppressed passion.

Angela could spend the rest of her life in that gaze.

"I think you could give me a lot of pleasure."

Her cue. A smile. Her hands landing on the firm planes of his pecs, her mouth lifted toward his. "I think I'd like to."

"But..."

"No." She put her finger to his lips, shaking her head, heart thudding in spite of her miraculous ability to act as if she were in total control. "We're here, Daniel, you and me. We're alive and we're together. This is supposed to happen. For both of us."

He closed his eyes, and for one second she thought he was going to balk. Then, slowly, remarkably, his gorgeous lips parted to kiss the finger she held there, their touch smooth and warm.

One kiss on one finger, and she was on fire with longing. *Steady.*

His mouth moved down to her palm, pressed a kiss there,

too. She let herself melt fully against him, and whispered, "You're okay with this?" just to be sure.

"Yes." He murmured the word without hesitation; his hand cupped the back of her neck and he bent to her mouth, his lips sure and sweet.

Angela's reaction was likewise without hesitation, likewise sure and sweet, begun and completed in the same word: *Yes.*

Her arms slid around him and explored the sweep of his back, the rounded power in his shoulders, the soft prickle of hairs at the nape of his neck, the thick tangle above them.

And oh, that mouth. Firm, warm, varying pressures and positions, so every kiss felt new. She closed her eyes, let her other senses lead, taking in the hard length pressed against her abdomen, the hands wandering over her, slowly descending the small of her back, stretching to the rounded swell of her bottom.

Angela moaned at the touch, the intimacy, the erotic promise, and something broke loose between them, turning the kisses hot and deep. She pressed her pelvis against him in a suggestive rhythm, over and over until they were both panting and desperate.

Clothes. She pulled up the hem of his shirt, bent to press lips to the firm wall of his abdomen, working her way up his chest, stopping to circle his nipple with her tongue, nipping gently, loving his soft *"oh"* of pleasure.

More. She shoved the material of his shirt higher. He reached to take it off, flung it onto the clean worktable. Angela slid her fingers inside his shorts to cup the soft handful of his balls, pressing the heel of her hand against the base of his penis.

Daniel held still for an endless second while she touched him, then groaned and threw his head back, eyes closed. It hit her suddenly: the poor man hadn't been touched by a woman in a year and a half. The realization shot her desire higher and hotter. He deserved this any way she could give it to him.

"Will anyone come in?" He murmured the words, swaying on his feet.

"I closed and locked up." She slid down his body to kneel at his feet, heard his brief gasp when he realized what she was going to do.

"You…planned this?"

"I was hoping." She lowered his biking shorts, anticipation growing as his erection came into view, material sliding down its length before it cleared him to jut up and out.

Free at last…

Mmm. His cock was beautiful, substantial without being frightening, golden and smooth, rosy at the tip.

She pressed her cheek against it, nuzzled his balls with her nose, then lips. Tipping her head back, she ran her tongue over his length, then let her mouth close gently over the head, holding for a few seconds, listening to his uneven breathing.

Then she gave him what he wanted, closed her lips firmly, moved forward, then pulled back, forward and back, tonguing him, sucking hard, then letting go, sucking hard again. His gasp of pleasure urged her on; she fisted the base of his penis, pulling the skin taut, used her other hand to caress his balls, feeling deep satisfaction and arousal of her own at his barely controlled excitement.

"Angela."

"Mmm?"

"If you keep doing that…"

"Mmm?"

"I'm not going to be able to…"

She paused for the rest of the thought. Not going to be able to what? Hold off coming? Get it up again? Stand?

"…make love to you the way I want to."

Make love? Not screw or ball or bang?

She peeked up at him. "How do you want to?"

"Slowly and sweetly, so I can look in your eyes and feel you with me."

Daniel. Something inside her split into two halves, warm and lovely on the one side, icy and threatening on the other.

Hands came under her arms and pulled her to standing. He kissed her mouth, her cheek, her forehead, her mouth again. "You are beautiful, Angela. Watching you with your tongue all over me…"

He finished the sentence with a low sound of pleasure that made her shudder and shove away the odd oil-water mix of feelings. "I'm glad you liked it."

"*Liked* it?" He chuckled. "Yes, I 'liked it.' A lot. Why are you wearing clothes?"

She glanced down at her top and skirt. "Gosh. I have no idea. How did that happen?"

"Don't worry. I'm on it. All over it, in fact." He ran his hands up her sides, dragging her knit top with them, then pulled it over her head. She shook her hair back, hoping he found her body at least half as sexy and wonderful as she found his.

One quick hitch and her bra loosened, her breasts felt cool air in a room usually jungle-like from the heat of the ovens. Then his mouth took her nipple, warm and insistent; he palmed her other breast at the same time, and she nearly fell over.

Her turn to moan, close her eyes, clutch his head and ride away on the sensations. She'd been too long without this kind of touching, without feeling skin on skin. How had she survived?

"Come with me." Daniel moved them, step by step, toward the back of the room. She didn't know where he was taking them and didn't care. She just wanted to feel him touching her more, touching her everywhere, so she could touch him back everywhere as well, every inch of his smooth skin and muscle.

Stacked paper sacks of flour hit the backs of her thighs. Somewhere in her lust-hazed mind it registered that flour packed solid might be about as soft as cement. Right then she didn't care, eased herself down, feeling the flour shift slightly underneath her, grudgingly accommodating her shape. She pulled gently on Daniel's shoulders, inviting him to climb after her, over her, hoping the bags wouldn't break or fall underneath them.

He put on a condom, pulled from some pocket she hadn't been keeping track of. Angela gestured and mimicked his previous question. "You planned this?"

"Like you, Angela, I was hoping." He lowered himself over her, his solid, beautiful body aligning itself to hers, up on his elbows to keep most of his weight off her. The feel of him touching her, toe to chin, both warmed her and made her shiver in delight. This was what bodies were made for. This was perfect. This was so right.

He lifted his head from the hollow of her shoulder and whispered her name, gazing at her as if she were the goddess of love and beauty.

Angela caught her breath, holding his eyes, unable to look away, mesmerized by their connection. *No, no, not love.*

He reached down to guide himself toward her. The head of his cock pushed against her opening. So intimate. So hot.

"Mmm," she whispered. "Come in."

Daniel pushed harder, another inch entered. Angela caught her breath, started to move, then stopped, forcing herself to be patient, to savor this. He closed his eyes briefly, let out a nearly silent *ohh*. Then the blue eyes opened again; he lifted and pushed powerfully, sliding into her wetness all the way, and oh, there was nothing like that first full slide inside. Her interior was alive with sensation, registering his thickness, his length, burning with excitement.

For a dozen heartbeats they lay still, joined, staring into each other's eyes.

"Angela," he whispered, "Thank you for bringing me back to life."

Sweetheart. Her heart swelled; she clasped his broad shoulders and tangled their legs, intensifying the pressure between them.

Wait... *Sweetheart?*

What the hell was she thinking?

Daniel started a slowly, lazy, movement, thrusting in deep, holding one, two, three, then circling his pelvis to stimulate her clitoris, pulling in and out to a lullaby beat, then doing it all again. And again. And again.

Oh, oh, oh. She'd never been made love to like this. So slowly, so sweetly, as if the contact between their bodies was all that mattered to him now and to the end of the world, while against all expectation, the leisurely pace only increased the intensity of her arousal. She was pushing back against each maddeningly slow thrust, making soft noises, fingers digging into his skin, her head lifting, then falling back, flour giving under the pressure.

Who had made the world disappear? There was nothing else but this man and what he was doing to her, nothing that she could take in except him, his body, his hard push inside her, the burning depth of her arousal and a slowly spreading deep, sweet ache in her chest.

What was happening? Was this—

No. *No.* Angela couldn't be falling for him. She couldn't be that much of an idiot. Not again. While she'd planned only to let him into her body, her foolish heart, not happy with only that much connection, was trying to invite him inside as well.

No and again no. He was a stranger; she was falling for a fantasy of him—the man who'd complete her life, rescue her from loneliness, protect her, adore her, spoil her and let her spoil him. The One, The Only. She'd stuck square Daniel into that round role without any deeper consideration than thinking he was hot. Love his body, yes, what he did with it, absolutely. But love him? No.

Choosing a life partner took much more than that.

Without realizing, her anger and confusion had made her movements more urgent, and Daniel responded, quickening his rhythm, using his hands to fondle and tease her breasts, bringing her arousal roaring back to life, more powerful than her worries.

"Ohh." She lifted her legs, locked them around his back to draw him in deeper, squeezed her muscles to hold his erection tighter with each thrust. She wanted him to come quickly, she wanted to get out of this situation before she lost the rest of her heart. The rest of herself.

Daniel lifted his head, tipped it back, eyes shut, mouth half-open, shoulders and neck straining. He was close. Oh, yes, he was close. And so, so hot.

She closed her eyes to block him out, which only made it harder to ignore the delicious sensations between her legs, the pull and slide of him inside her. No, no, no, she'd been lying; she didn't want this over with, she wanted it to go on and on and on.

Her desire built into certainty. She was going to come with this man inside her, and had an awful feeling she'd never be the same again.

A low moan escaped her. She pushed harder against him, lifting her hips, close to orgasm, then closer. Sweat broke out on her body, the wave crashed over her, hot and inevitable, leaving her gasping and crying out.

"Angela, oh, man, I feel you coming." He held still while she pulsed around him, then dug his hands underneath her buttocks, thrusting hard, his breath coming fast and hoarse next to her ear.

"Angela." He whispered her name, then stiffened and gave the sexiest groan she'd ever heard, pulsing inside her over and over.

Sweetheart. She was full, full everywhere, full of him, between her legs, in her head, in her heart, on her skin. *Daniel.*

Oh, God.

She was lost. Her only hope was that Daniel would also freak out over the power of what they'd shared.

He lifted his head from her shoulder, sated and blissful, eyes glowing blue, smile hovering over his masculine mouth, increasing both her tenderness and her jitters. This was not the face of a man who deeply regretted breaking his vow. This was the vibrant face of a man with potent sexual energy.

Planning seduction had been easier when he'd seemed adrift and miserable. Now Angela was in danger of being swept away by her reaction to this new, confident masterfully sexual Daniel, the same way she'd been swept away by Tom.

Except, no, damn it. Angela was not that same woman. This Angela was fully conscious of her patterns and perils. She'd set out to help Daniel break free, and in the process free herself to start dating men again. Mission accomplished.

But…she'd learned a lesson. No more fast and furious. From now on she'd take things slowly, date around, and stay away from flour sacks until she was sure the man was worthy of her feelings.

Which meant she'd need to extract herself from this situation right now, before she—

"Angela."

"Yes?" She avoided his eyes. Looking into them was still too intense, still made her feel too much more than their brief association warranted. The urge to escape strengthened.

"I didn't expect this. I didn't think this would—" He shook his head, gave a wry laugh. "It's too soon."

"What do you mean." *Too soon!* Angela was hopeful now. Daniel had been struck with a guilty conscience. He'd slide regretfully out of her body and say a fond farewell, sorry, but he couldn't see her again for at least six months. He'd slipped once, yes, but a promise was a promise….

It would hurt. She knew that. In such a short time she'd gotten to like this man unnaturally much. But separation was for the best. She'd have time to calm down, to date other men, get her feelings for this one in perspective. This would be the best and healthiest rejection she'd ever had.

She was ready. *I can't believe this happened, Angela. Sex was a serious mistake we can't repeat.*

He opened his mouth. The words were on their way. She couldn't wait. At the same time, God, she dreaded them. The bitterest pill…

"I can't believe this happened, Angela," he whispered, right on cue. "You're so sexy I'm already hard again."

9

"LOOK WHAT I have." Bonnie came into Angela's shop holding the most gorgeous bouquet Angela had ever seen, all her favorite colors and flowers: fuchsia roses, red gerbera daisies, orange spray roses, burgundy mini carnations, peach Peruvian lilies, all against lush greens in a black glass vase.

"Oh, how gorgeous, Bonnie. You've outdone yourself." Angela came out from behind the counter, drawn out of her irritable navel-gazing by the sophisticated riot of color. "Are these for your display window?"

"Nope. They're for you."

"Bonnie." Angela glanced up at her, taken aback. Bonnie had brought over flowers now and then, a few stems she thought Angela would like, and which added a lovely touch of color and style to the bakery. But this...this bouquet would cost a fortune, and Angela was pretty sure Bonnie was in no shape to part with a fortune. "This is so sweet of you, Bonnie, but you don't have—"

"Of me?" She grinned mischievously and set the bouquet on top of Angela's display case where it looked absolutely stunning. "I put it together, that's all I did."

"What do you mean?" Something wasn't making sense about this, but Angela was exhausted, hadn't slept well, and had a million things on her mind today—new recipes, sales calls, wondering how her samples had gone over at Slatewood, and of course lots of quality freak-out time over what had happened last night with—

"Daniel."

Angela blinked at Bonnie. How did she know? Had she heard or seen something?

"The flowers, Angela." Bonnie spoke impatiently. "They're from Daniel."

"From…Daniel…" She stared blankly.

"Is this hard for you to understand? Would it help if I wrote it down?"

Angela snapped into focus. "Thank you, I got it."

"You got it." Bonnie narrowed her eyes. "What is this, a bad thing to get the most lavish, expensive bouquet I've had ordered in weeks? I'd be turning cartwheels."

"Because you know how, Ms. Former Gymnast."

Bonnie's too-thin features tensed into concern. "What happened, Angie? I assumed they were I'm-falling-for-you flowers. Are they an apology? What did he do? If he was horrible to you, I'll—"

Angela put a hand over Bonnie's clenched fist. "He wasn't horrible. I'm horrible."

"*You* did something horrible and *he* sent you flowers?" She put a hand to her chest. "Oh, my God, does he have a brother? A single father? Widowed grandpa? I'd be all over that."

"How would I know?" She couldn't keep the exasperation from her voice. "I don't even know the guy."

"Okay, but by this time you must have at least an instinct about him."

She did. An instinct that was shouting very loudly. *Run away, stupid! Falling for someone means vulnerability, and vulnerability means being wide open to betrayal and pain!*

Making love—his choice of words had been absolutely appropriate—with Daniel had been so much more intense than she expected. Stupidly she thought she could just seduce him into a fun, playful hookup they'd both enjoy, maybe do it again a few times, maybe eventually settle into a relationship, maybe get back on their feet, romantically speaking, by getting off their feet. But no. That was for other women, stronger women, women in charge of themselves and their emotions. Not saps like Angela whose subconscious must still be in adolescence, equating kissing a guy with commitment. Making out with an engagement ring. Sex with a wedding night.

"I like him." She shrugged and tried to laugh, but the effort fell flat under Bonnie's scrutiny. "We have a good time. He's fun to talk to."

"Uh-huh. Fun to talk to. Right." She fussed with a pink rose, pulling the stem up and replacing it. "I happened to see him leaving here last night when I was on my way upstairs. He looked pretty happy. A little disheveled."

"Oh, well. He'd biked over."

"Mmm-hmm." Bonnie turned abruptly, folding her arms across her chest. "He had flour on his knees."

Angela's face immediately grew hot, and a smile she couldn't control had its way with her mouth. She'd still had flour in her hair this morning. "I can explain that. See, he dropped a contact lens, and we were on the floor together looking for—"

"Bus-ted," Bonnie sang. "So what happened?"

Angela slumped against her counter. "It was really, really nice, Bonnie."

"And this is bad how?"

"I flipped out." Angela gestured helplessly. "I don't want a relationship. I don't even want to *want* one. It's too soon. I can't get hurt again. This was supposed to be fun. Light and easy. And it's…"

Bonnie raised her eyebrows. "Not?"

"Not." Angela let out a long sigh. "I know myself. I attach

too much importance to the tiniest feelings. I need to chill out and be friendly and not assume we're getting married and that soon he'll be cheating on me, all because last night we… got flour all over us."

"Was it good flour?"

"It was." Angela closed her eyes for a second. "The best flour I've ever worked with."

Bonnie grinned about as wide as Angela had ever seen her. "You're doing fine. Your instinct is right to play it cool. Guys are all over you for sex, but if they get the slightest whiff of I-want-more, they bolt."

"Ooh, so can I get Daniel to leave me alone if I demand serious commitment?"

"Bingo. Wait, no." Bonnie's brows dropped into confusion. "That might not work with this guy. Those are *really* nice flowers."

"They are." Another sigh.

"And I don't think you want him to leave you *totally* alone."

"No. I don't know." Angela put a hand to her forehead. "This is all making me so tired. I need about a million hours to work everything out and start fresh."

"I know, honey." Bonnie gave her shoulder a squeeze. "I feel that way about once a month. It will be okay. Just be honest about what you feel, to yourself and to Daniel."

Angela peeked at her. "Um. Like you are with yourself about Seth?"

Bonnie's turn to sigh, only it came out more like a growl of exasperation. "If I though honesty would work, I'd try it. But right now the best weapon I have is to tell myself very firmly and with one hundred percent conviction that I am over Seth and to believe it. It works and I like it. Okay?"

"Yes. Okay." Angela hugged her. "Maybe I need to try that."

"You know, it's not a bad idea. Makes dealing with the

gorgeous, lovable bastards much easier. For once, you get to keep power on your side."

Angela nodded. Yes. Exactly what she wanted. Exactly. To make sure going forward that when it came to relationships, power remained on her side.

DANIEL WAS FLYING. Technically he was on his bicycle, but the way he felt, the way his muscles were working, sorry, gravity didn't apply. Hills were nothing; he was Lance freaking Armstrong crossing the Alps in record time.

He was on his way to see Angela.

What a sap he was. Her name had been playing in his head all day at work, and all last night. He'd woken up this morning with *An-ge-la* still spinning in his mind, her image tattooed in his memory, a goofy smile on his face.

Last night she'd freed him. He'd gone over to A Taste for All Pleasures certain that his life was about to change, that she held the key to whatever new door would open for him. He hadn't necessarily intended to make love to her, certainly not in the back room of her bakery. But she'd been so sexy, so seductive, that innocent sweet face coming closer, her long slender fingers breaking the cookie in pieces and feeding him, the soft touch of those fingers on his mouth.

All at once, understanding had hit him, clearer than ever, though he'd been inching his way there for a while. Jake had been right. This was his life, and it was okay to live it. Kate would understand, he was sure of it.

Mostly sure of it.

But he'd made his decision, had made incredible floursack-moving love to Angela. Twice. And instead of being racked with guilt afterward as he'd feared, Daniel had felt an enormous weight lifted, not only of grief, but also of an unwanted responsibility. Freedom from the hold Kate had on his life and on him that he'd started out cherishing, and ended up resenting, without being aware that he did.

Kate had been a lovely woman, and he'd adored her. She'd been the embodiment of what he needed at that time in his life. But he no longer needed that. Lying awake last night, finally facing hard truths he should have faced years ago, he'd also recognized that for the last couple of years he and Kate had together, being with her had felt less and less safe and comforting and more and more restrictive as he matured. The hardest truth of all was facing that their marriage might not have been a happy one.

In sharp contrast, being with Angela was thrilling and unpredictable and, most importantly, not already mapped out on her terms. Daniel couldn't wait to go forward with her, discovering and defining each other and themselves as a couple for as long as they lasted, whether that was a week, a year or forever.

Yeah, he was flying. He turned onto East Olive Street, cold wind streaming over him, body warm from working hard. He hoped she'd liked the flowers, that her incredible smile had lighted her face—and probably the whole shop—when she saw them and realized they were from him. Had she lain awake last night thinking about him the way he'd lain awake thinking of her? Thoughts that had gotten him so hard, he'd had to reach under the covers and get some relief, while imagining her doing the same. In his fantasy, she was unbearably sexy touching herself. He'd like to see that. He'd like to see everything, do everything with her—on the big metal table in her bakery kitchen, bent over a couch, sitting in a chair, lying on a beach somewhere, in the woods. And yes, in bed. Long lazy hours under and over and tangled in the covers and in each other.

His cock was stirring just thinking about it.

Damn, how different the world and his place in it looked right now than it had two weeks ago. He couldn't even imagine how he'd thought that previous life worth living. The clichés were true: the air seemed fresher, colors truer, Seattle seemed to have inched closer to spring. He probably had animated bluebirds and little red hearts circling his head.

He chained his bike to the rack outside Come to Your Senses and bounded up the steps, helmet in his hand, through the front door and straight into the bakery, passing an old woman in a hot pink suit.

Angela was bent down arranging odd-looking tarts of some pale yellowish fruit in the display case when he went in. Her long hair was swept back from her face and cascaded in a stunning fall visible through the glass. Her face looked rosy and sweet. His heart nearly stopped. God, she was beautiful.

A glance around told him his flowers weren't there. Bonnie hadn't brought them over yet? She'd promised to deliver them immediately after he called that morning. He'd hoped Angela would have them here in the bakery with her, where she could see them all day and be reminded of him. Maybe they were in the back, commemorating a certain stack of flour bags?

"Hi." He let the simple word sound as intimate and tender as he knew how.

"Oh." She jumped up, flustered, glanced at him guiltily, glanced away. "Hi, Daniel."

Not quite the welcome he'd hoped for. "How's the day going?"

"Fine." She nodded, clutching an empty tray she'd used to unload the tarts. "Thanks for the flowers."

"You're welcome." He stepped toward her counter. Something wasn't right. She'd thanked him in a flat voice, without enthusiasm. Not that he needed her to gush over him or his gift, but…

Well, yeah, actually he'd hoped she would.

"Anything wrong?"

"No." Her eyebrows were raised too high, she was shaking her head too rapidly, her smile was too forced. "Nothing.

It's all good. Good to see you, too. That was Marjorie you passed on the way in, in pink. She comes in every day to buy breakfast for the following morning. She's a sweetheart."

"Oh…" He was dumbfounded. This was not the reception he expected. What the hell happened between now and last night? He'd left her, melty and clinging, responding to his kisses as helplessly as he'd given them. He'd made her come twice more, once during the second time they had sex, once after that with his mouth. She was insatiable and uninhibited, without losing that sweetness that had drawn his heart in to a much greater degree than he expected.

Daniel hadn't thought he was in any shape to fall for someone else this soon. But some relationships started that way, with a—wait for it—bang, and some took time to grow. This one was definitely a banger.

"Heard anything from your boss?" She was chipper. Chipper and brittle. He wanted to leap over the counter, grab her into his arms and kiss her until she melted back into the woman she was meant to be with him. The woman she'd been last night, free and confident, funny and bold.

"Larry took the samples home today. He leaves first thing in the morning for Detroit. I won't talk to him until the end of the week."

"Okay. Thanks. So…" She gestured to the cupcakes. "Need anything today?"

He leaned on the case. "Actually, yes. I need something today."

"Oh." Beautiful pink spread over her face as she caught his meaning. "We're out of that."

"Really. Hmm. I got the impression last night you had plenty in stock."

Her color grew higher, her lips softened into the beginning of a smile she didn't let spread farther. "Not on the schedule today."

"No? Want to tell me why not?" He let the silence build,

hoping she'd either tell him what was going on, or drop some hint he could figure out.

"It's just…I don't…I'm not…"

Daniel's eyebrow went up. His heart started squeezing painfully. She couldn't pull back now. Not after what they'd shared the previous night. "Just tell me, Angela. What's going on?"

"I can't do it now. Not yet."

Did she mean… "You're, uh, indisposed this week?"

"No. No, not that." She shook her finger, as if she needed to make very sure he got the negative nature of her statement.

He got it. The sick feeling was now spreading through his heart and into his stomach. "Okay. Then what's the matter?"

"It was too much. Too fast."

Daniel flashed back to last night, Angela feeding him the cookie, her gaze pointedly sexual, telling him her favorite part of baking was giving people pleasure. "I am pretty sure you set the pace."

"Yes. Yes, I did. I'm not trying to dodge responsibility for that."

Dodge responsibility? Were they talking about tax payments? "I'm not holding you responsible, Angela, I just want to understand. You wish it hadn't happened? That we hadn't been together last night?"

"Yes. No." She let her shoulders slump and looked down. "No, I don't. I can't quite wish that."

Thank God. "Tell me more? I'm still not getting it."

"I don't want to be vulnerable to you. I can't be." She raised her head and he was shocked by the agony in her face and voice.

"Oh, honey." He reached over the counter, touched her chin briefly. "Can we go somewhere and talk about this? Somewhere there's not a counter between us?"

"I need a counter between us."

He laughed. "You're afraid I'll attack you?"

"No." She peeked up at him, smile pulling at the corner of her mouth. "Afraid I'll attack you."

The lead ball in his stomach dissolved, replaced by a giddy bubble of happiness. This woman had a powerful hold on him, in an entirely different and healthier way than Kate had. Power that left him paradoxically free.

"Hmm. How about I'll give you my word that if you attack me I'll fight you off as hard as I can."

"Well..." Her smile bloomed. "There's an apartment upstairs we all share. We can talk there."

"Sounds good." Her own place would work really well for him, but a shared apartment would be better than standing here. With the other four "senses" most likely working in their respective shops and studios, upstairs would probably be empty.

Angela summoned Scott from the back to work the counter while she was out, and they took the elevator up to the second floor.

The extra apartment reminded Daniel of a dorm room, only cleaner: mismatched worn furniture, and not much of it, prints on the walls, mugs abandoned on the counter, a recycling bin half-full of beer bottles. Still, it managed to be comfortably welcoming. And thanks, he presumed, to Bonnie Blooms, the plants in the place were thriving.

"Would you like a beer?" Angela was heading to the kitchen.

"Sure, thanks." He chose the god-awful black-and-white couch to sit on, in case she decided she could risk sitting next to him. He'd have to work hard to keep his hands off her, but he couldn't imagine sitting on opposite sides of the room as if they were lawyer and client at a business meeting.

She appeared from the kitchen carrying two bottles of Elysian Ale, smiling determinedly through an obvious case of jitters Daniel immediately wanted to cure with a long, slow back rub, oil making her soft, smooth skin glisten under his fingers…

Think of something else. "I saved you a seat."

"Thanks." Angela pinned herself to the arm rest on the other end from his. He wanted to laugh. Hadn't they been in a frenzy for each other's naked bodies about twenty-four hours ago?

"Cheers." He twisted off the cap to his beer and took a long sip. "So tell me what's going on."

"I want to keep this casual." She gestured back and forth in the empty space between them. "Yesterday was sort of… intense."

"Mmm, yeah." He injected the words with wistful fondness, gazing off into the imagined distance. "And so hot. I was thinking about it and you all night long. When you were lying there naked, with your—"

"Ahem." She sent him a look, amusement lurking in the back of her expression as he'd hoped. "Not helping."

"No?"

"Not at all."

"You'd rather I lied? Like this?" He made a sick-to-his-stomach face. "*No,* I don't want to do that again, either. Next time we'll skip all that disgusting touching and just wave to each other."

"Daniel." The beginning of laughter showed through her warning tone. "I'm being serious. I don't want a relationship right now."

"Define relationship."

"Okay. For one, I don't want to date you exclusively."

"No?" He had to fight to keep his tone light after that punch to his gut. "Who else you got in mind?"

She frowned. "No one yet."

Thank You, God. "But if you meet someone else, you want to be able to date him?"

"Yes. Yes. Exactly. I'm not ready to settle down. I'm not ready to assign a label to any feelings I...might have for you."

Skittish. Afraid of feelings he suspected—hoped, prayed—she *definitely* had for him. "But you think I am ready?"

"Oh." That gorgeous blush rose, making him want to taste her skin, as if it had just turned strawberry-flavored. "I don't know, really. I just thought. I mean last night you were so..."

"So what?"

"Sweet. And tender, and..."

"So were you, Angela." He lowered his voice, put his hand along the back of the couch and leaned toward her. "We both were. It was amazing. We jumped right in, wide open to each other."

She blinked. "Oh. Well, yes, I guess so."

"You guess so."

"And then this morning those flowers..."

"Hmm." He pretended to look confused. "Did Bonnie put a ring in the bouquet? I didn't ask her to."

"No, no." She giggled in the midst of trying to look earnest, which was totally adorable and also managed to be sexy because he was that crazy about her. "But—"

"I sent you flowers, because I like you, I think you are amazingly hot, and on top of that, I really enjoy your company." He dared pick up a strand of her hair, tugged it gently, let it fall and followed it with his hand, onto her shoulder. "More than that, Angela, you showed me how I was hiding behind the promise to Kate, hanging onto my grief to avoid having to start over."

"I'm glad. I wanted to do that for you." She took a deep breath, put her hand to her chest. He tried very hard not to focus on it. Her breasts were full and tempting him under her clinging peach-colored top. "When you told me about Kate, I don't know, something snapped. I got angry at her, and wanted to help you in a way I wasn't able to help myself for way too long."

"Pity f—?" He stopped himself from saying the word.

"No, no, not like that." She shook her head, then suddenly started giggling. "More like a freedom f—"

He cracked up, too, not because it was that funny, but because they both needed a release from this crazy tension. And while they were both laughing, it seemed utterly natural to slide his hand across her shoulder, and pull her toward him for a kiss.

And apparently it seemed utterly natural for her to respond.

He was going to stop soon. Otherwise, it would look as if he'd tricked her up here with promises of chaste talk and was now attacking her the way he said he wouldn't.

So he'd stop kissing her.

Right now.

Or…maybe in a second.

Or maybe never.

Her mouth was warm, sweet, willing, he couldn't get enough. His hand itched to explore, to stroke the soft swells of her breasts. But if he did that he really wouldn't stop. He'd make love to her right here on a couch so ugly that flour sacks could only be an improvement.

Somehow he channeled superhuman powers and decelerated their kisses, ending with his lips clinging to hers for one endless moment before he pulled them away.

Her eyes were wide, dark, her color high. She was so lovely he had to turn his head or he'd reach for her again.

"I thought we weren't going to do that." Even her voice was sexy—low, breathless, everything about this woman turned him on.

"We weren't." He reached for his beer, something to distract him, a desperate attempt to cool himself down.

"We did, though."

"I take full responsibility."

"I didn't exactly stop you."

"Not exactly." He grinned, took another sip of beer.

"No." She was smiling now, too.

"So. Now." He furrowed his brow. "What were you saying?"

"I have no idea." She shook her head helplessly. "You mess up my brain."

He reached back in his memory. Something she'd said needed explaining. "What did your ex do that made you want to get me out of my promise to Kate?"

"Ah. A sweet little story." She took a long swig of beer. He even loved that she chugged it straight from the bottle, with a face that should always be behind a crystal champagne flute. "Let's see. Tom was the rich golden boy, rich family, et cetera. I was the poor little Greek girl."

"Half-Greek."

"Half-Greek. And not really poor. Just not in his class."

"Undoubtedly not. And I'm not talking social class, so that's a compliment."

"Thank you." She beamed at him and he wondered if he'd ever felt this weird combination of being buoyed up and relaxed around anyone else. "His parents were horrified by me, which I suspect was what he wanted. God, I'll never forget my first dinner *chez* Hulfish."

"Fun?" He wanted to go back in time and keep her away from any and all humiliation.

"First of all, the house is a mansion. I walked into this place…you should have seen it. Marble and velvet and fine art, such incredible taste and style in every inch of it. I felt like poo on the carpet no matter how many times I went."

"You're much more than poo on a carpet to me, Angela."

She giggled. "It gets worse. Tom told me to dress casual. So I show up in a reasonably decent outfit. His mother is outfitted for a freaking royal wedding, probably in a dress some designer made for her. It was absolutely stunning. And of course she has that up-and-down you-are-so-lacking look perfected."

"What a sweet woman." He was appalled, not only at the description of these horrible abusive people, but also at the wistfulness he wasn't sure Angela knew she still exhibited.

"She was dragon bitch from hell. Anyway, so during the whole evening, she pointedly brings up topics she's sure I have nothing to say about. 'Tosca was so wonderful at La Scala, remember, Mark? You know that opera, don't you, Angela?' And of course I'd say, 'No,' and she'd wrinkle her nose and repeat 'No' as if the word smelled bad, and I did, too."

"*Why* did you marry into this family?"

She pressed her lips together, lines forming on her forehead. "The weird thing is? I loved them all. That was who they were, and they played themselves absolutely flawlessly. I guess I hoped some of that sophistication and taste would rub off on me, and I'd fit in with them. To some degree that happened. I did become crazy about Tosca. But I hoped they'd eventually accept me for who I was, too."

"How did that work?"

"Uh…" She made a face. "Not well. So anyway, we married, we honeymooned, we settled into a huge house that other people cleaned, and I thought I was happy. In retrospect I think I was still just in awe."

"Retrospect is smarter than we are. Too bad."

"Very too bad. Anyway, living the dream, telling myself I was happy, yada yada, then he started staying out late, blah-blah-blah and ended up leaving me for a woman so perfect I am pretty sure she never even passes gas."

"Ah. That's not good." He shook his head in concern, tamping down anger at the jerk who'd hurt her, and who'd made it so hard for her to trust him now. "Eventually she'll float away and then where will he be?"

"Ooh, I hadn't thought of that." She pretended to consider seriously while giggles shook her. "Maybe he'll tie a string around her and keep the other end on his wrist?"

"She'll be very popular around Thanksgiving."

Her eyebrows went up. "For?"

"Macy's Parade."

He hadn't seen many miracles before, but he was seeing one now. Angela, convulsed with laughter. Loud, free laughter, in waves of such beauty he wanted to videotape her so he could play this precious moment over and over again. Even better, he wanted to find ways to get her to that joy often. With him. For a long, long time.

"I like that version much better than thinking I wasn't enough."

His smile suffered instant death. "Angela, the guy is a total jerk who used you."

Her mouth opened, closed. "No. He was…I wasn't in his league."

"You'd want to be? The Jerk League?"

"No, no, I mean he was so—"

"Untrustworthy."

"But he was—"

"Selfish."

"Maybe, but he was also—"

"An ass."

"Okay, okay. He was." She gestured and let her hand fall onto the ugly cushion between them.

Daniel grabbed her fingers and held them, wanting fiercely to let her know that whatever had happened in the marriage wasn't her fault. She was not only enough, she was…everything. Everything he'd ever wanted. And he didn't even know it until he met her, and started realizing what had been missing from his relationship with Kate, bless her and God rest her beautiful but rather rigid soul.

"So because your ex was an untrustworthy selfish ass it follows that I am, too?"

"No. No, no." Her eyes were stricken. He wanted to kiss both of them, get the smile back on her face. He wanted to protect her from everything, a macho side of him he hadn't known he possessed. Probably because Kate hadn't needed him. Not as much as he'd convinced himself he needed her.

"Why do you have to stay away from me if I'm nothing like him?"

"Oh, Daniel." She sighed, features bunched in confusion. "Tell you what, when human emotions become totally logical, let me know."

"Point taken." He brought her fingers to his lips, kissed her palm, the soft skin of her wrist. "So we slow down now."

"Yes, please."

He kissed her forearm, the inside of her elbow. "No more sex?"

"Not…often."

He cupped her face with his hands, met her halfway so their lips were an inch apart. "No more kisses?"

"Some of those," she whispered. "Sometimes."

"Like now?"

"Well…"

He didn't wait longer, brushed her lips with his, heard her catch her breath and deepened the pressure—only slightly. *Angela.* She'd seduced him out of his stupor, out of his depression and misery and into a new life and new depths of emotion that felt so promising and so right he was half ready to tell her he was falling in love with her.

He *was* falling in love with her. And because of some other creep who treated her like crap, he had to pretend he wasn't?

Daniel kissed her again, as chastely as he could manage with insides ready to burst into flames, and then he let her go.

This time.

"I stopped."

"Yes." She smiled wistfully and didn't move away. "Thank you."

Daniel did move away. Picked up his beer and prepared to settle in for a nice platonic discussion. She wanted to go slowly? He'd play along for a while. But understanding what she was feeling only made it more important he act now, to do for her what she'd done for him. Free her from the hold this creep still had on her self-esteem. Seduce Angela into realizing Daniel was not her ex-husband or any part of her past.

But he was hoping to be her future.

10

BONNIE KNELT to re-re-rearrange bright tulips in a cream-colored bucket. Only two customers so far today, three phone orders and one wrong number. Not good. April was supposed to give people spring fever, make them want life and color and good fresh smells around them, especially in a year when spring was taking longer than usual. But April had been rough on Bonnie Blooms, as had been March, February, January…

Instinctively, Bonnie had started economizing in little ways. Not so much with her flowers, but in her life. Less meat, more cheap starches for dinner. Canned fruit instead of fresh. Cheaper beer and wine when she did indulge. No more fancy manicures, coloring her own hair…nothing drastic, just caution. Something would happen to turn her business around. April would turn to May and June, weddings would start happening in greater numbers. And in the meantime maybe she'd come up with an advertising gimmick to steer more flower-buyers her way. Maybe she could use the rather risqué picture Jack had taken of her, the one he'd promised would make Seth wild with jealousy, to make an ad for her flower shop. She could post it outside gentlemen's clubs and barber shops. *Hey, bay-bee, come pluck my petals.* Disgustingly sexist, but it might just come to that.

Tulips looking perfect enough for her taste, Bonnie wandered back to her register. With no one around, she felt free to open the drawer under her counter and take out the picture Jack had slipped under her apartment door, probably in the middle of the night, given the weird hours he kept. She studied it, grinning. Jack had captured her in a heavy-lidded Marilyn Monroe smile that somehow worked, even with her all-American freckled face and average features. He'd posed her on an off-white drape in a way that rounded her too-skinny hips and brought out respectable length in her legs. Over her nipples, between her legs and outlining her body bloomed deeply pink moth orchids that emphasized the rosy tones in her skin. He'd even managed to make her small breasts appear lush and promising, their curves peeking out from behind the petals.

She looked nothing like the way she thought of herself, and she absolutely loved it. Jack had a real gift, an eye for coaxing out the best in his subjects. He was good in bed, too, though they never got serious enough to call theirs a relationship. After the initial passion was spent, they'd settled happily back where they belonged, as friends.

Voices outside her store entrance made her jump and slide the picture under the register. She was not ready to share it. Jack had seen this side of her, but it wasn't something she thought the others knew about, except Seth, of course. But she was not up for being teased about something that delighted her so much, and yes, the gentlemen's clubs would have to wait, too.

The voices neared and became recognizable. Seth's lazy baritone, and the horrendous nasal squeak of the lovely and no doubt talented Alex-ahn-drah, who he'd apparently had up in his studio again today, and was now kissy-kissing goodbye. Afternoon delight maybe? How nice. Bonnie was happy for them.

Super-duper happy.

What a mistake to go out for drinks with Seth on Saturday night. They'd had such a good time together, been relaxed and happy, the way they used to be when it seemed as if the future existed only for them. At least that's what *she'd* been thinking back then. His thoughts had probably been along the lines of *sex, food, more sex, sleep, even more sex...*

She'd woken up Sunday morning feeling upbeat and energized for the first time in way too long. As soon as she'd realized why, her mood had turned leaden and cranky. Something had to get her out of this horrible lethargy. She'd worked hard to get over Seth, and had succeeded, she thought, enough to agree to be part of Come to Your Senses. But being in close proximity to him like this, day after day for the past year—too many of her feelings had threatened to return. The only way she'd ever get over Seth permanently was to fall for someone else. Maybe Angela was right, and she should try dating, because she was starting to feel as pathetic as she was.

"Hey, Bonnie."

"Hi, Seth." She made herself look sweet as honey, ready to sting like a honey bee. "Have a productive afternoon?"

"We did a lot of good stuff, yes."

"Really." She looked him over. "Must not have been that good. You can still walk."

"Walk?" He sauntered over to her counter, leaned on it. Too close. She stepped back. "What, you thought we'd been drinking?"

"No, dear." She fluttered her eyelashes at him. "I thought you'd been screwing."

"Well, well." A slow grin spread over his sexy mouth. "You jealous?"

She gave a derisive raspberry. "Of course not. Why would I be?"

"I dunno, Bonnie." He reached out before she could rear back, and his fingers gently brushed the corner of her mouth and down her chin before he took them back. "Why don't you tell me?"

Um...no.

She scrubbed at the spot he'd touched, as if the contact had bothered her. Which it had, but not the way she wanted him to think. "Did I have a crumb on my face?"

"Nope. You had a face on your face."

"I've had that for a while."

She waited for his next retort. To her surprise, he started looking around at her flowers as if he'd just realized he was in her shop, and the fact fascinated him. Bonnie held still, watching. Something had to be making Seth uncomfortable, for him to drop the teasing.

"Hey, Bon…"

She waited, waited some more, then prompted, "Ye-e-es?"

"I dunno."

"Do you really like this woman?" The words rushed out before Bonnie could weigh the pros and cons of asking. Now that they had, she could see the ratio clearly: one hundred percent con. She dropped her eyes miserably to the counter. Maybe she'd convinced Seth she wasn't jealous before, but this would sink her.

"Alexandra? She's okay." He'd turned his head back; she could feel his gaze. His hand landed on her shoulder. Why was he touching her so much? "I'm not involved with her. I told you that. It's the truth, Bonnie."

Relief, which she was immediately furious at herself for. Whether he was or wasn't boinking the sexy squeaker shouldn't matter to her at all. "You don't owe me that."

"Maybe not. But I don't want you thinking something about me that isn't true."

"It was a natural assumption. Don't forget, I know you.

She's over here all the time up in your apartment. You bought her those flowers."

Ugh. She sounded like a jealous girlfriend. Why couldn't she act sanely around this man?

"The flowers were for her mom's birthday. She paid me back." He was looking at her intently now, hazel eyes somber. Very un-Seth-like. "I hired her to sing one of my songs."

"Ahh." Bonnie tried to pretend she was interested in this from a purely musical standpoint. "I didn't realize you'd written one for Minnie Mouse."

Meow.

Seth cracked up, head hanging down, as if he were trying to hide the laughter. When they were dating, Bonnie would nuzzle under his neck, make him lift up to share the fun with her. She'd asked him about it once, but he'd only shrugged and said it was just what he did.

"Something's stuck under here." He had his finger on a corner of her picture, which hadn't disappeared all the way under the register.

"Oh. No." She jabbed her thumb down hard to pin the photo to the counter before he could pull it out. "That's mine."

"Yeah?" He was grinning, and she knew right away she'd lose this battle. Seth was as determined to get what he wanted as she was. Plus he was stronger. "Show me."

"No, it's private."

"Really." He tipped his head. "Looks like a picture."

"It is a picture."

He frowned. "New boyfriend?"

"Well, well." She lifted an eyebrow, trying to grin the way he had been only a minute ago. "You jealous?"

He imitated her responding raspberry perfectly. "Of *course* not. Why *would* I be?"

They were both laughing now, Seth trying to pull the picture out, Bonnie hell-bent on keeping it hidden.

Finally he grabbed her wrists, held them together in one hand and drew the sheet out with a flourish.

"Ha! I win! I've—" He let go of Bonnie's wrists. "Holy… Look at this."

"I've seen it." She became suddenly involved in examining her fingernails, wishing she wasn't secretly pleased he could see her like that, the way Jack saw her.

"Look at you."

"Don't need to. I was there."

"Did Jack take this?"

"Yup."

He narrowed his eyes. "When?"

"Last night."

Seth put the paper down. "You were with him last night?"

"Yup. Stark naked. Nothing he hadn't seen before. Though, hmm, back then I don't think we ever did it in flowers."

He was furious. Growling. She loved it. Take that for parading Alex-*ahn*-dra around. See how it felt.

Immediately she was ashamed of being so vindictive. Seth brought out her best and worst sides. And everything in between.

But if he didn't still care about her, he wouldn't mind that she'd posed naked for Jack. Not to the point where his jaw was clenched tight enough to break his teeth, the way it was now, a sure sign he was trying very hard to keep a rein on his emotions.

"Bonnie…"

If she could only get hold of that rein, cut it through with one triumphant stroke.

She lifted her chin. "Yes, Seth?"

"Are you with Jack now? Again?"

"No." Her voice gentled as his had. They could only torture each other for so long. "Just posing for a shot he wanted."

"I bet he did."

"Oh, and you've never imagined Alexandra naked?"

"Never!" He smacked his hand on the counter. "Never would I do such a thing."

The lie was so blatant he couldn't possibly have expected her to believe it. Sure enough, he was staring maniacally, lips pursed, eyebrows up.

She laughed again, loud and long. Even better, he joined her. Seth was too damn fun. And sexy. And utterly exasperating.

He was looking around the shop again. She braced herself. "Hey."

"Hey, what, Seth?"

"You ever notice we still act like a couple sometimes?"

She couldn't help the residual snort of laughter. "Gee, no. I've never, ever noticed that. Not at all."

"Yeah, me, neither." He was grinning at her, and she was still grinning at him, and then both their grins faded at the same time, at the same rate, while something a lot less funny and a whole lot richer started to take its place.

No. She was not letting him take her down this same damn road yet again.

"Hey, Bon-bon."

"No." The word came out more brusquely than she intended, but she didn't soften it with any others.

"Let's go out tonight. Dancing or something. You and me."

"I'm busy."

"Tomorrow."

"Nope."

"Next day?" He tipped his head, doing the puppy-eye thing that used to work without fail. Today, it got him nothing.

Okay, not nothing, but she was staying strong. "Next day lots of stuff happening, too."

"The weekend."

"Even more."

"You don't want to go dancing with me."

She sighed and took back the naked picture, opened her drawer and shoved it inside.

That was the trouble. She desperately wanted to go dancing with him. But then what? There were three completely predictable possibilities—one, they'd drink, dance and have a great time, but the evening would end up being completely platonic, and she'd be perversely and painfully disappointed. Two, they'd drink, dance and have a great time, he'd make a move, and she'd rebuff him and go to bed frustrated and upset. Three, they'd drink, dance, have a great time, he'd make a move and she'd give in, then hate herself afterward for weeks.

See? Not a good plan.

"No, Seth. I don't want to go dancing with you."

"Okay." He tapped smartly on the counter and turned away, but just before he did, she got a glimpse of real disappointment on his handsome face. A glimpse of disappointment and of pain.

11

Angela followed Daniel, risking her very life biking behind him because she kept being distracted by his rather gorgeous butt, muscles she knew to be very strong and very solid, working to power his cycle down Pine Street. They were on their way to the Seattle Art Museum to hang out in the wacky sculpture garden, then maybe get some ice cream.

Daniel was clearly honoring his word to take their relationship slowly. An after-work bike ride during which it was downright dangerous to get any closer than about three feet? Decidedly platonic. Sculpture was cerebral. Ice cream, with no alcohol to decrease inhibitions? Lamb-innocent.

So. He'd respected her concerns and she was safe.

Yes, sir. Safe as a snowball in Antarctica. A raindrop in the Amazon. A fireball in hell.

Wonderful. Ju-u-st wonderful.

Left onto Second Avenue, right onto Union, left on First. Daniel pulled up next to the rack closest to the museum, where they secured their bikes and walked around the building to the Olympic Sculpture Park, built on waterfront property reclaimed from industrial use, a green area for strolling and viewing art. The park was peaceful and surprisingly quiet, given its downtown location.

They strolled down the grassy steps of the Bill and Melinda Gates Amphitheater and wandered around and through a series of undulating metal sections of wall comprising a sculpture called *Wake*. Angela stopped between two of the massive shapes, gazing up at the sky outlined between them. She had to keep her gaze on the sky because after about three seconds of vainly trying to lose herself in a sculptural experience, a warm, male body had come up behind her. Close behind her. Painfully, wonderfully, magnetically close.

"I'm not really art-savvy." His voice was low and too near for comfort, but plenty near enough to make her want to lean back into him, feel his arms sliding around her, encasing her in his warm strength, to savor the gentle pressure of his lips against her neck. "But I love this sculpture. It's awe-inspiring, both in size and concept."

"Yuh." She barely managed that brilliant analysis without choking on it. Her shoulders had pressed into his firm chest for one brief moment. Had he swayed forward or had she swayed back?

How was Angela supposed to keep power on her side when around this man she turned instantly and rather pathetically slavish? Was she genetically doomed to being a simpering doormat? Yes, she'd rejected further intimacy with Daniel, a powerful choice, but what good did that do her if she spent every second in his presence craving it? Maybe it had been a mistake to say slow down. Maybe she should have said stop.

And yet...

Even the idea of not seeing Daniel again sent a blade of pain through her.

His hand landed on the small of her back, then slid away, the tips of his fingers barely brushing across her bottom. "Let's move on."

No, stay. Put your hand back where it—

Yes. Move on.

They toured the rest of the garden, sweet air drifting in

from Puget Sound, the temperature truly springlike for the first time that year. Sun would be nice, but Seattle's residents knew better than to hope for miracles too often. It made those miracles all the more special when they happened.

"I think this one's my favorite." He pointed to what looked like a bizarre rubbery pink unicycle wheel, except where the seat should have been, a wiry bunch of bristles shot up, like an old-fashioned twig broom turned upside down. "My grandfather had one of those."

"Typewriter eraser or giant sculpture of one?"

"Ha. Eraser." He shifted and his hand bumped hers; she had to stuff her fingers into her jeans pocket to keep from grabbing it and holding on. "Imagine having to erase."

"Imagine." She was imagining something very different. Namely, what it would feel like to make love to Daniel outdoors, with a lovely sea breeze caressing their bodies.

This was nearly hopeless.

"Were you close to your grandfather?"

"I barely knew him." His arm made contact, stayed pressed against her shoulder for a split second, then he took a step away. It was all she could do not to follow. "He died when I was ten, we didn't visit often."

"Oh, I'm sorry." At least Angela could stop lusting long enough for genuine sympathy. When she imagined Daniel as a child, he was always sad, quiet and alone, which put fault lines in her heart. When she pictured her own childhood, she was always centered in a giant clump of loving—and loud—relatives.

"How about you?" He touched her forearm. "Wait, I know this one. *Big Fat Greek Wedding.* Yes, you were close to everyone."

"Figuratively and literally. Parents, brothers, grandparents, aunts, uncles, cousins, nieces, nephews…"

"I envy that."

She turned to him, shading her eyes from the sun setting behind him, lighting strands of his hair gold. "You were lonely."

"I guess, yeah. For family anyway." The words came out hoarsely, a difficult confession. Automatically Angela's hand began to extend toward him, and she had to push it back to her side.

"How about now?"

"Right now?" His hand had no compunction about completing its journey across the small space between them; it pushed aside a lock of hair breeze had sent tumbling across her forehead. His fingers lingered, slid down the side of her cheek.

Angela nearly stopped breathing. "No. I meant. In general. Do you see your mom and dad? How about Kate's family?"

His ex-fiancée's name had the intended effect. Daniel turned and started out of the park, toward sculptress Louise Bourgeois's father-son fountain on the corner of Alaskan Way and Broad Street.

"Not really and not really. My parents are my parents, and I think it was too hard for Kate's family to keep me around. But when you grow up without something, not having it feels like more of the same, not a big hole."

They stood for a minute by the fountain, watching the jets of water covering first the statue of father, then son. Angela felt a deep longing to go back in time and give child-Daniel what he didn't have.

Oh, Angela. Bad enough she couldn't stop wanting another taste of his body. Now she wanted responsibility for his whole psyche, too?

"I never asked if you had brothers and sisters. I'm guessing not?"

"Not." He took a few steps away to view the fountain from a different angle. Angela managed to hold her ground for about five seconds before she followed him like a puppy. "How did you get along with your brothers?"

"Well, for the most part." She laughed, thinking of the four of them, Alex, Chris, Nick and Stephan, all older by five years or more. "They actually morphed from being my biggest tormentors to my biggest champions and protectors. We're in touch, very loving, but I wouldn't say we're extremely close anymore. They have their own lives, all married. Alex is in Portland, Chris is in Chicago, Nick and Stephan stayed in Iowa."

"Any of them bakers?"

"Hardly. Two farmers, a stockbroker and an insurance agent."

"Would you care to sit on an eyeball?"

"Why I'd love to, thank you." She sank on the seat extending from the back of one of the oddly disturbing pair of giant stone eyeballs on the sidewalk. Daniel sat on the one next to her, crossing his long legs. She wished he'd move farther away. Or much closer. She didn't seem to be doing so well with this middle ground.

"I'm curious." He extended his arm along the back of his eyeball. "Why expand your offerings at the bakery when the goods you're selling now seem to be doing really well?"

She gathered her lusting thoughts into platonic cohesion. It was very important Daniel understand.

"I told you about the high-end European bakeries I fell in love with on our honeymoon. Walking into a place like that is like stepping into another world. As if you've left the ordinary part of yourself and your life behind, and you're part of something beautiful, special and exclusive, where there are no pesky annoyances or mishaps or conflicts." She glanced at him, awkward and vulnerable, sharing what probably sounded like a completely over-the-top reaction to a place selling flour, fat and sugar. "I'd like to give people that experience. And hell, I'd like to live there part of every day, too."

Daniel listened attentively as he always did, but not as if

he were enjoying her description. Rather as if it troubled him, which troubled her. "Funny."

"What is?"

"You sound the same way talking about this bakery ideal as you did about Tom's family."

Angela felt a jab of annoyance. "But this bakery would be mine. I never could have said that about his family."

"Okay." He was clearly unconvinced. "Don't get me wrong, I think the idea is great. I was just wondering why that one particular aspect, the sophistication, is so important to you."

Angela shifted irritably on her eyeball. "Because it's wonderful and special. Anyone can make cookies."

"Not like yours."

"Well, thank you." Instead of pleasure at his compliment, more annoyance. "But I want more than that."

"I hope you get what you want, Angela." He was watching her; she was watching the fountain. "I really do."

But... The word was so obviously left off the end of his response he might as well have shouted it.

Angela stayed still, trying to quiet her feisty inner warrior, recognizing that this conversation was grating on a very sore point, nothing Daniel could be aware of. Now that she'd finally dragged herself out from under Tom's influence, she did not need another lover casting aspersions on her goals and ambition. Which made it even more important that she stay away from Daniel physically, so she'd keep her overly romantic nature at bay and pay close attention to what kind of partner he'd really be.

Because, as she'd discovered in her marriage, all the sexual attraction in the world wouldn't sustain a relationship if the foundations of respect, understanding and support were missing.

"OKAY, SO THEN after the museum and ice cream on Tuesday, you went out for coffee yesterday, and tea and sandwiches today, and he said goodbye each time having totally honored your request to take things slowly."

"Yes."

"And you are miserable because...?"

"I'm *not* miserable." Angela stroked another coat of mascara onto her eyelashes. She and Bonnie were in her bedroom getting ready for a night out dancing with friends. "What makes you think I am? This is exactly what I wanted. I'm completely—"

"Miserable." Bonnie turned this way and that in front of the mirror, smoothing her leopard-print minidress. "Quick question, how long have I known you?"

"Bonnie." Angela sent her an exasperated look. "I don't know. Eight years. What does that have to do with anything?"

"You don't think after that long I'd know when you're not yourself?"

"Who else would I be?"

"Gee, I dunno. Maybe Ms. Fooling Herself? Or how about Ms. I-Don't-Know-How-to-Admit-I-Never-Wanted-Platonic-With-This-Guy-Anyway? Or, no, no, plain old Ms. I'm-In-Love-and-All-Shook-Up."

"Stop that." Angela capped the mascara and tossed it back into the wicker basket she kept on top of her dresser for her everyday makeup. Bonnie was making her extremely cranky, mostly because she was probably right. Spending time with Daniel had been wonderful torture. Every time he'd sat near her or part of his body had bumped, brushed or slid past hers, which had happened with truly agonizing regularity, she'd sailed either into memories of their lovemaking or fantasies of future lovemaking. Telling herself how important it was to get to know him really well before they continued a sexual relationship didn't work at all on her subconscious, which continued to be slavishly infatuated. Even her dreams were invaded. She'd decided there was nothing more depressing than waking up blissfully in a man's arms after a night of exquisite passion, turning to kiss him…and waking up for real, alone in bed after another night of solo snore 'n' drool.

She couldn't go on like this. Something had to give. The obvious two options were to tell Daniel she was sorry but she couldn't see him anymore, or to invite him somewhere private, rip his clothes off and hop on for the ride of a lifetime.

Neither was preferable. She still hoped some miracle third solution would present itself so she could have her chocolate-cupcake man and eat him, too.

"Okay, I'm sorry." Bonnie fluffed up her beautiful red hair, which was dead straight and refused to fluff, but which never stopped her trying. "Or no, I'm not really sorry. But I do understand. And I'm one to talk, since I've got some of the same issues with Seth. But I've been working like mad to be honest with myself. This month has been weird between us again."

"I sensed that."

"I know, I know. Going out for drinks with him was a mistake. Letting Jack take that picture was a mistake." She turned from the mirror, biting her lip. "I do want you to know that I appreciate you looking out for me, Angela. For warning me I was playing gasoline-covered chicken with the big bad bonfire again. It really did make a difference. I think I'm doing better, not letting him get to me so much. At this point my feelings for him are mostly a habit, and I'm determined to break it."

"Bonnie, I'm so glad to hear you say that." She hugged her friend, who had doused herself with so much perfume Angela had to hold her breath. Bonnie never did anything halfway. "You are really brave. I know how painful it is to let go of something you thought was right."

"No kidding." She wiped away the beginning of a tear. "God, don't make me cry, my eyeliner will run and I'll look like a coal-mining raccoon."

"Right. Never mind. Forget the sentiment." Angela released her, backed away with her hands up. "You're not that great. Really annoying, in fact."

"Thank you. Perfect." Bonnie checked her makeup in the mirror, heavier than Angela would ever wear it, but on Bonnie it always looked cool. "Now. Because I am no longer fooling myself over my feelings about Seth, you must therefore face your feelings for Daniel, too."

"Oh! Look at the time." Angela held up her wrist, which had no watch on it. "We have *got* to go or we'll be late. You know Jack hates when we're late."

"Angela…"

"Busy, busy, busy." She shoved Bonnie out of the way and took one last look in the mirror at the sexy black mini-dress she'd bought shortly after her divorce and hadn't ever felt like wearing. Tonight, something in her had said what the hell. It wasn't racy by club standards, just by hers. Solid black with wide shoulder straps, it had beaded fabric covering her breasts, which were on display more than in her usual wardrobe, and fell in flirty folds to midthigh. A good dancing dress.

They were going to a club called Noc Noc on Second Avenue, one of Bonnie's favorites. Angela had to be in the right mood to enjoy crowds, drinks and deafening noise. Tonight she was. She wasn't quite sure what had happened to her mood, why the skimpy dress had been the evening's only choice. Why Ms. Stay-At-Home was excited at the idea of going to a club Bonnie said was lit and decorated like a vampire den. She felt reckless. Maybe a little desperate. Going dancing with friends was the perfect outlet.

Out in the hallway Jack waited, clearly impatient, looking extremely hot in jeans and a close-fitting shirt in blues and grays.

"What were you two doing, weaving cloth for your—" His dark eyes lit on Angela. He did a comical jaw-drop and clutched his chest. "Angela. My God. I think my heart just stopped."

Bonnie giggled. "Doesn't she look amazing?"

"You do, too, Bonnie." He sidled up to her and ran his hands down her arms. "But I expect blatant sexuality every day of the year from you, so it wasn't a life-threatening event."

"I understand." She kissed his cheek. "Thank you, dear."

"You're welcome." He took each of them gallantly by the arm. "A couple of my friends are meeting us there. Seth isn't sure he'll make it but he'll try. I invited Demi, too."

"Gee, let me guess." Bonnie spoke in a low voice, glancing around. "She's busy."

"Not surprisingly, yes, she is." Jack led them to the elevator. "Ready for a night of dancing debauchery?"

"Absolutely. Lead the way." Bonnie leapt, ballerina-like, into the elevator and spun around. "Hey, can we tell Noc Noc jokes?"

Jack and Angela exchanged glances. *"No."*

On the first floor, Jack propelled them past the locked entrances to their darkened businesses. Angela shivered stepping out onto the sidewalk. Not so much because the air was chilly again, which it was, but because the night felt sparkling new and full of exciting possibilities. What those were, she had no idea. But instinct told her she was in for a really great time.

Noc Noc turned out to be everything Bonnie said: crowded, hot and boisterous, dimly lit orange and red, vampire den, yes, or the inside of an S&M dungeon. But the food and drinks were good and not expensive, the booths large and comfortable, the dance floor not impossibly small and the bartenders friendly and quick.

All the ingredients for a fabulous time.

Except Angela wasn't having one. She drank cocktails with weird names and too much sugar, ate too many tater tots, a specialty of the house that arrived in large amounts, hot and crisp, for only a few dollars. She danced with Jack, with his friend Blake, with Seth and with a couple of random guys who flattered her with their obvious attraction. She chatted, flirted mildly, laughed at jokes, made some of her own, went through all the motions, but the anticipation of having a really wonderful, special evening was falling flat. Something was missing. Something that would make everything fall into place, that would make her feel…right.

She hated to admit it. Hated to. But she knew what that thing was. That thing that would complete the evening here tonight, or anywhere else tonight. Or any other night.

Finally, after her third cocktail, she mustered her courage—or simply didn't care anymore about anything else—and shouldered her way out of the crowd, heat and noise, into the blessedly fresh air outside. By the time she reached the sidewalk, her cell was in her hand.

"Daniel?"

His voice was lost in the shrieking laughter of a nearby group of girls.

"What?" She clamped a hand over her free ear. "I can barely hear you."

"I said hi. Where are you?"

"Noc Noc."

"Okay. Who's there?"

Angela burst into alcohol-enhanced giggles. "No, no. I'm on Second Avenue at a *club* called Noc Noc."

"Oh, yeah, I've heard of it. Couldn't figure out why you'd call me this late with a knock-knock joke."

"Unless it was a really good one." She was smiling so hard that in a few seconds her cheeks would start hurting. Daniel was what she'd really wanted, what had been missing this evening. If she had any doubt, the wave of joy and contentment at hearing his voice erased it. Maybe she'd had one drink too many, but all her reasons for staying away from him seemed contrived and artificial, born more of fear than reason.

"Come dancing with me." She didn't ask, she ordered.

"Wow." He laughed nervously. "I'm…not much of a dancer."

"Oh." She felt herself wilting into disappointment. Having come to the brilliant realization that Daniel was what her evening needed, it selfishly hadn't occurred to her he might not feel the same. "You can come out and *not* dance."

"I could. But Angela…" His voice lowered. Angela took a few more steps toward a quieter part of the street. "Jake isn't here."

"Oh." She tried to figure that one out. "So the apartment would be lonely if you left?"

He chuckled. "Not quite what I was thinking."

"What were you think—" *D'oh.* She knew what he was thinking. Point the first—he didn't want to come out tonight. Point the second—Jake wasn't home.

She got it.

A cold breeze whipped down the block, chilling her skin, moist from perspiration.

"Angela?" His voice had remained low, but she could hear him clearly, as if there were no way her ears would miss what he was about to say no matter how much noise was around her. "How about coming to dance with me over here?"

12

ANGELA STOOD outside Daniel's building, taking deep breaths. The trip over to his house by cab seemed to have sobered her up completely, for which she was grateful. If something happened between them tonight—okay, something would happen between them tonight—she wanted to be clear-headed enough to use good judgment. To understand what she was doing and why. Because she knew without a doubt that one look at him would make her want to—

The building's front door pushed out and Daniel was standing there, tall, solid and handsome, grinning as if he'd never stop. It was hard to associate this vital man with the pale imitation who'd walked into her bakery for the first time two weeks ago. "Thought you might change your mind if I didn't come out and drag you in. God, you look amazing, Angela."

She'd been right. One look and she was ready to jump his bones. She'd just put it that bluntly and be done with it.

"I'm…I was…" She started giggling. Not because anything was funny, but because he looked good enough to devour and she was so happy. No, she hadn't been having fun at Noc Noc. Fun was now, fun was Daniel. He lit her up as if she was made of neon.

"You were what? I'm thinking you were on the verge of running away."

"No, no." She peeked at him coyly. "I needed time to prepare myself for the awesome experience of seeing you."

"Ahhh." He reached for her hand, drew her into the stuffy little space between the outer and inner doors. "And were you fully prepared?"

She whistled silently. "I nearly passed out, but managed to recover."

"Glad to hear that." He squeezed her hand, looking her up and down, sending shivers of anticipation over her body. "I'm going to need more time to recover from seeing you. You are stunning. I've never seen you dressed like that."

"I never dress like this."

"You should. Often." He ran his hand down her bare arm. "But only around me. Otherwise I'll have to fight through every man in Seattle to be with you."

"Ha." She gave him a skeptical look while her insides did a dance of pleasure. "It's just a dress."

"Oh, no. It's not just a dress. It's a body, also, the kind that makes men forget they're civilized beings. And…" He touched her cheek in that sweet and tender way that managed to get her hot because she was as depraved as hell. "It's you."

"Oh. Well. Thank you." She couldn't stop smiling, even having just sounded struck stupid. Any second she'd start laughing. The man turned her completely goofy.

"Ready to go up?" He twined his fingers with hers. "No thoughts of running away?"

"Let me check." She held his gaze, blue and warm and so, so wonderful. "No. Not one."

"Okay, let's go." He turned to the door. And stopped. "Oh, God. I came down without my keys."

"Oh, no!" Jake wasn't up there. They were stuck.

"Our date curse continues, Angela." He sounded more amused than upset.

She was the opposite, hastily scanning the row of apartment buzzers. "Can we bug someone to let us in?"

"Nah, I don't want to bother people at this hour. We'll just wait until someone comes along."

Angela stared at him. Something was weird about this. Didn't he want to be upstairs with her as desperately as she wanted to be up there with him? "Who's going to come by in the middle of the night on a Thursday?"

He shrugged. "Gee, I don't know."

"Daniel!"

"Yes?"

"You'd rather be down here in this stuffy little box than upstairs with me?"

"I don't know. What did you have in mind?"

"You are kidding, aren't you?" She started laughing.

"No, I'm completely serious." His voice was anything but. "What did you think the two of us might do upstairs in an empty apartment that would make getting out of here worthwhile?"

She couldn't stop giggling. "If you don't know, then—"

"Tell me, Angela," he whispered. His face was serious now. Apparently she could stop giggling. He cupped the back of her head, holding it steady. "Tell me."

Heat flooded her body. Pictures came to mind immediately, then words, and then a wicked idea. "I thought maybe we could sit on your bed together."

"Close together?"

"Yes, yes, very close." She moved until she was nearly touching his body with hers. "The lights will be low, maybe some music on. Something soft with a good pulsing beat in the background."

"And then what?" His hands bumped hers. Their breathing was audible in the small space. Their chemistry was as palpable. Angela nearly regretted her plan.

Nearly.

"Then I'd like to take my dress off." She put her hands to the solid planes of his chest, her heart beating so hard it felt as if it were about to burst out of hers. "And then I'd like to take your shirt off. And your pants. And everything else."

"Mmm, I'm really liking this plan."

"And then I'd like to do…something." She pulled at his shirt until it exposed his skin, pressed her lips there once, twice, gave a slow lick with the very tip of her tongue.

"What kind of something?"

Angela slid her hands over his hips, down his thighs. "A kind of something I bet you've never done with a woman before."

"Oh, my God." He spoke on a groan. "What? Tell me."

She was about to hit him with her punch line—read Mother Goose poetry to you—when her fingers encountered a bulge in his pocket. Not the normal are-you-glad-to-see-me bulge. A bulge that felt like—

"Keys!" Oh, he was *so* busted. And he'd totally upstaged her joke.

"No, no, tell me what you were going to—"

"The keys are in your pocket." She smacked the bulge and folded her arms across her chest.

He gasped. "I had *no* idea."

"You just wanted me to talk dirty to you."

Daniel chuckled and dug out the set. "Can you blame me?"

"Yes." No, not in a million years. "You will have to make this up to me, Mr. Flynn."

"I will, I will." He fit a key into the door. "Come upstairs and I'll show you how."

"Well." She pretended to consider, thinking that this kind of teasing silliness had been a big part of her family life and completely absent from her relationship with Tom. What had made her think she could find happiness with him, with his family, in that totally foreign environment? Being with

Daniel felt like coming home again. "I guess you could do that."

He escorted her inside the building and they climbed the carpeted stairs in silence that was full of promise, full of unexpected emotion. Angela had no need to fill the quiet with chatter as she always had with Tom. She and Daniel had gone from silly teasing to this totally different kind of intimacy easily and with mutual understanding.

Bonnie was right. She was falling for him. Hard. Yes, too soon, yes frightening, but by now undeniable. And if Daniel turned out to be a jerk and crushed her heart, so be it. She'd live to love again.

She would.

That fact was probably obvious to most everyone on the planet, but for her it was a lightning bolt of realization. She didn't have to have power over Daniel. That had been the wrong place to focus, the wrong way to approach him, with gloves on, hands up in strong defense.

She'd always had and always would have power over herself. And that was all she needed.

They entered his dimly lit apartment; he closed the door behind them. "Do you want anything? A drink? Something to eat? Glass of water?"

"No. Thank you." Angela walked to him, feeling more whole and sure than she ever had. "Just you."

He wrapped her in his arms, took her mouth with his. She responded, and without warning or preamble they caught fire, immediate, blazing and disorientingly hot. They devoured each other's lips, pulled at each other's clothes, greedy for the feel of skin, then stumbled through the living room and tumbled onto the couch, not even willing to go a few yards farther into his bedroom.

"Daniel." She gasped out his name, grabbed his shoulder to pull herself on top of him.

"Wait." He stopped her.

Wait for what? What was he doing? She pushed hair out of her eyes and saw him rolling on a condom. Thank God he had enough of his brain working to remember.

"Now." He spoke urgently, pushed himself against the back of the couch and opened his arms.

"Yes, now," she whispered, and climbed onto him, grasped his penis eagerly and guided it just barely inside her.

Ohhh. They made the sound together, gazing into each other's eyes. She lifted off, let her weight drop again. Another half inch.

Ohhh.

Up again and down, another inch that time as he stretched and filled her. Brief pause, then next time down nearly all the way, loving his hissed intake of breath, the way his eyes narrowed into fierce enjoyment of her movement. Up so he was almost free, another pause then she sank deliberately until he was all the way in, both of them gasping at the pleasure. Angela rested there, listening to their breaths catching, feeling more beautiful and desirable than she could ever remember, and more comfortable in her own body, knowing that Daniel wasn't thinking of the woman he wished she was, but of her, Angela Loukas, naked and crazy about him.

The urge to move became strong; she used the muscles in her thighs to lift and lower in a regular rhythm, dropping her head, eyes closed to savor the feeling. She took it slowly, landing with him deep inside her, circling her hips to stimulate her clitoris, delaying gratification of her need to ride him harder. She wanted to be in this moment as long as possible, to be aware of Daniel and her feelings for him. Now that she was no longer afraid of them, no longer in denial, she wanted to take them out and examine them in as much detail as she could.

Up…and down. Up…and down, feeling him, feeling for him, until Daniel grasped her hips, urging her on. Angela gave in, increasing the pace and the arousal, throwing her head back, parting her lips, giving herself over to the delicious thrust and pull. His hands left her hips, arrived on her breasts, warm palms caressing her.

The touch sent her even higher, she used more strength, wanting him in and out faster, harder, keeping awareness of Daniel over her body's animal need for release until that need took over and she panted his name, clutching his hard shoulders, tipping her pelvis forward so her clitoris ground against his pubic bone on every thrust.

Yes. *Yes.*

Her breaths grew shorter, her muscles threatened to cramp. She couldn't stop, couldn't interrupt the sensation of being entered over and over, the slow and perfect rise to ecstasy.

Seconds before her climax hit, she opened her eyes, and found him watching her, his jaw tight, muscles taut with his own pleasure.

"Daniel." She barely got his name out, felt her body flush. She was close. "I'm going to come."

"Angela."

"Right now." She arched back, let the wave burn over her, felt him grab her and work his hips in a wild loss of control that bounced her up and down.

"You are so sexy." He spoke through clenched teeth. "You're making me insane."

Oh, Daniel. If she was sexy it was because he made her feel that way, every minute she was with him.

"Good," she whispered. "I want you insane. And I want you to come inside me."

He did, with a brief shout of ecstasy that tensed his body and flooded his skin with color. Joy swelled her heart and her throat. This man…

His eyes opened, bright blue, sated and happy. He pushed hair from her face, leaned in to kiss her, then brought her back against the couch with him and kissed her some more.

And then more, and after that, more—long, sweetly passionate kisses.

Ohhh, she loved this. Amazing sex with an amazing man. And look at her. Angela Loukas was okay, blissfully okay, and still in control of herself and her emotions.

"I'm really liking the take things slow angle." He stroked her hair, her arm, her back. "I wasn't so sure the last times we went out, to the museum and so on, but yeah, right now I'm a total convert."

She rolled her eyes, head resting against his shoulder. "Um, that's great, Daniel."

"Seriously. This is the best platonic date I've ever had. You were absolutely right that it would be better if we took things slowly until—"

"Okay, okay." She laughed; she couldn't help it. "So that didn't work."

"It couldn't. It's too strong between us."

She lifted her head, feigning confusion. "What is?"

"Uh." His eyes narrowed; he looked supremely uncomfortable. "You know. 'It.'"

More laughter. "Chicken."

"Yeah?" He poked her shoulder. "You define it then."

"I will." She snuggled in again; his arms came around her, making her feel protected, delicate and small. She was none of those things, she was a tough Amazon warrior princess, but right at this moment burrowing safely against a large, warm male body felt perfect. "That's easy."

"Yeah? Tell me. What draws us to each other?"

"All that platonic lust."

"Really."

"Uh-huh. Nice and simple. I want you, you want me, we do it platonically, and then it's over. That's why when we finished, I immediately climbed off you, got dressed and left."

"Ah. Good. Okay, then. Thanks for explaining that."

"You're welcome." She smiled against his skin, inhaled him shamelessly. "Anything else?"

"I was thinking…"

"Mmm?" His hands were absolutely delicious, spreading and kneading the muscles of her upper back and shoulders. She wanted to hire him as her personal masseuse. And sex slave.

"Maybe we should keep on using each other like this. You know, many more totally platonic dates where we screw and then leave each other right away. What do you think?"

She kissed the swell of his pectoral, happiness fizzing away inside her. "It's not a bad idea."

"There's only one problem."

"What's that?"

"I'm not sure I feel that platonically about you."

"No?" She blinked in surprise. "You're kidding, right?"

"No. In fact." He held suddenly still, which made her breath stop instinctively. "Angela…"

She waited, on a thin edge between hope and apprehension. "Yes?"

"I'm falling for you. You're…I mean when I'm with you, I…I've never felt…" He let out a breath of frustration. "I'm a guy, sorry."

"No, no, I heard you." She felt suddenly completely calm. This was right. She was falling for him too and that was completely okay. "You said, 'Angela, when I'm with you the world is a better and brighter place, and I've never been able to feel so myself and at the same time so connected to someone else.'"

"Wow." He laughed, shaking his head. "That's exactly what I said. You have excellent hearing."

"I feel that way, too." She did. Crazy about him and also strong and intact in herself.

His laughter faded. He put gentle fingers to her chin and drew her mouth near; they kissed again, but with a different kind of passion, the passion of two people who know there is nothing in the world more important or right at that moment than kissing each other to seal an emotional bond.

So she kissed him in that beautiful, sweet…

Um…sweet…

Ooh, not so sweet.

"Angela?"

"Mmm?" She was suckling the skin of his neck, brief bites of total abandon.

"I think we're about to get platonic again."

"Oh, yes." She made her way back to his mouth. "I think so, too."

"Not here, though." He invited her off his lap, then led her into his bedroom. "Here this time."

She looked around curiously, clinging to his hand. "Oh."

"It's not much but it's home."

"No, no, it's really nice." She rushed to reassure him. "Like a cozy…jail cell."

"Wait, really?" He appeared dumbfounded, eyes dancing. "White-on-white-on-white isn't your thing?"

"White-on-white-on-white with gray bicycle." She pointed to it, leaning against the wall, then did another slow spin. "You should get Bonnie to do up an arrangement of silk flowers."

"Flowers?" He squinted at her in disbelief. "I'm a man! You forgot this soon after I was inside you?"

"Hmm." She moved over to the bed, climbed on and tipped her head to look at him, thinking she'd never had this much fun in her life. "Remind me?"

"I guess I better." He grabbed a condom from his bedside table drawer and settled beside her; she welcomed him with hands leisurely stroking his chest, then his abdomen, down to his penis, which began to swell under her touch. Daniel knelt beside her, so strong and male, while his eyes watching her fingers were lit with warmth. She loved that dichotomy, his powerfully masculine physical presence, and his sweet, funny and kind nature.

He was growing hard, solid and tempting under her fingers. "Ohhh, yes. I'm remembering now. Male. Right."

"Glad to hear that." He rolled on a condom, then moved over her with typical grace to suckle her right breast, doing his Daniel-magic, getting her desire to lift its head and say, *Ooh, goody, again?*

Yes, yes, again.

Her left breast was next, honored and lavished with adoration that made her hips gyrate in anticipation of what was to come their way.

Except what came their way first was his mouth and his tongue, probing with gentle, wet touches that ratcheted up her breathing and made her body squirm with impatience.

Another sweet nip from his lips, then a long warm trail from the base of her opening up to her clitoris, setting nerves alight along the way.

"Oh. My. That is…" She closed her eyes, basking in the sensations. "Wonderful."

"You taste so good," he whispered.

His tongue again, touching, probing, leaving unsatisfied places here, then there, increasing her torture, and her desire. "Daniel."

"Mmm?"

"You're driving me crazy."

A deep chuckle, another light flick of his tongue across her clit. "Good."

"No, not good. I want." Her voice sounded odd, urgent, her hands scrabbled over the covers. She was slightly disoriented, and wasn't sure she should be. "I want…more."

"You'll get it." He kissed her reverently. She didn't want reverence. She wanted carnal, she wanted wild, she wanted the full length of his tongue, or his cock inside her. "In a minute."

She whimpered. "That long?"

His fingers joined in, teasing the outline of her sex, passing over her labia, spreading them, then tracing her opening while his lips barely tasted her clitoris, again and again.

Angela was going to scream. She was going to open her mouth and scream bloody murder. She hadn't ever been made this hot with so many teases, so few touches, so little certainty. She loved it and she hated it. She wanted him to stop and she wanted him to keep going.

"Please." God, she was begging. She'd never begged. Where was her power now? What had happened to keeping herself—

"Oh!"

Daniel pushed a finger inside her at the same time he lowered his mouth and worked her in earnest.

Angela's hips lifted off the bed by themselves. She heard herself making guttural, foreign sounds. Her hands reached to clutch his hair; her body writhed. She couldn't hold back. Whether she wanted to or not, he was going to make her—

"Oh!" Again she cried out, the orgasm slamming into her, second one always more intense. Over and over the waves came and she lost control, lost herself. "Daniel!"

A cry for help, as if she were going to drown in the feeling, which it seemed she might.

Then his weight on top of her, his lips on hers. Angela opened her legs instinctively, still pulsing with pleasure, pleasure that increased as he slid inside and moved urgently, almost roughly. She tilted her pelvis to take him in deeper, wrapping her arms around his upper body, breaths coming out nearly as sobs. His thighs slapped against hers with each thrust, his shoulder muscles strained. When he climaxed he whispered her name.

In answer came his name, followed by those three terrifying and important words, shouting so loudly inside her head, it was all she could do to keep from saying them out loud.

She'd seen the edge coming and had been unable to resist, had gone sailing over without any means of slowing or stopping herself.

Daniel, I love you.

13

ANGELA STARED AT her baking schedule for May, hand poised over her mouse. Lavender éclairs should come out of rotation; they were labor intensive and hadn't been selling well. If they'd been a new recipe for cookies or bread, they would have been history weeks ago. She'd kept them on for two reasons. One, because new products sometimes needed an extra nudge and she'd like to give them a chance. And two, because she was stubborn and determined, and they'd come to symbolize her dreams for A Taste for All Pleasures' future.

That was probably laying a little too much responsibility on an éclair.

She used her mouse to highlight the text: lav-en-der é-clairs. Time to be brave, sensible and practical.

Click. They were gone. See? Easy.

No problem. She was proud of herself.

Urgh. She put them back.

Apparently it was an indecisive day.

Angela had woken up after uneasy dreams in which Daniel had made love to her, smiling, then shoved her off the bed and shouted "done," which ushered in the next of what turned out to be a line of sexy, naked women curving around his block. The relief when she realized she'd been dreaming had faded while the queasiness remained. Daniel hadn't called all day, and her message on his cell had gone unanswered. She knew it didn't have to mean he'd gotten sick of her already, but…

The office phone rang, making her jump. *Flynn, Daniel* on the display. Hmph. Apparently he'd finished the line of women.

"Hello, Ms. Loukas."

"Hello, Mr. Flynn. How goes the day keeping Slatewood safe from the forces of evil?"

"Complicated. An employee turned off her virus software to download something yesterday and forget to restart it."

"Uh-oh." Angela cringed. "Anything happen?"

"Yup." He sounded exhausted. "The forces of evil accessed our central data bank."

"Oh, no! Oh gosh." Angela immediately felt tenderly protective of his company's data. No wonder he hadn't called. Though really, he could have… "Can you do anything?"

"Ha!" His tone was worthy of Captain America. "You doubt my power?"

"No! No, of *course* not."

"We caught it in time, in fact, the security systems in place worked just the way they should have, and our department got a big pat on the back. But it's been hell getting there."

"I'm sorry. But that is wonderful, congratulations." She swivelled her chair away from the computer. "I bet that woman is relieved."

"Rebecca?" He chuckled. "You might say that. We've been glued together all day."

Angela swallowed, not loving that image, and hating that she immediately associated a woman with why she hadn't heard from Daniel all day.

Calm down, Angela. Her dream meant nothing. As did the fact that Tom's affair with The Princess had started this way, with innocent mentions of how closely they worked together.

Tom was not Daniel. And vice versa. Rebecca was not The Princess. Angela hoped. "Glued why?"

"She's terrified for her job."

"Right. Of course." She tried to sound sympathetic and thought she'd done a good job. Sort of. "What will happen to her?"

"Wrist slap, that's all. I've been trying to protect her from the worst of it. She's really talented and the company needs her. I do, too, she's been a big help to me. So I really didn't want to see her swing for one mistake, even a bad one."

Angela unclenched her jaw. "You are very sweet."

"She brought me brownies. I'll do anything for a woman who gives me brownies. Or—"

"How old is this woman you'd do anything for?"

"I was going to say, or a woman who gives me cupcakes." He spoke gently. "There is only you, Angela. Believe me. "

Pleasure and sheepish relief poured over her like warm honey. She leaned back in her chair and grinned lovingly at the ceiling. "Really?"

"Re-e-ally." His voice took on a suggestive tone that made her smile harder.

"Am I pathetic for making you tell me?"

"You were hurt by a schmuck, Angela. It will take time to trust me."

The rest of her tension fled from the oncoming rush of goopy happiness. Daniel had understood her neuroses instead of blaming her for them. Imagine that. "I think I need to ask for something else, a little more reassurance."

"Go ahead."

"Well…" Her grin turned naughty. "If I told you I was sitting in my office in a miniskirt with no underwear on would that make you think about Rebecca?"

His breath hissed through his teeth. "Um…no."

"And if I told you that my hand was slo-o-owly making its

way down between my legs, would you be interested in that image?"

He groaned. "Angela, I have to go to a meeting in three minutes. I don't think it would be appreciated if I walk in with the Eiffel Tower in my pants."

"No?" She had to turn the phone away so he wouldn't hear her laughing. "Mmm, I'm spreading myself wider. Wide open for you, Daniel. Can you picture that?"

"Yes. *Yes.*" His frustration was obvious. "You are torturing me."

"Gosh, I am *so* sorry." She waited a beat before giving a sexy moan.

"What now? What?"

"I just put my finger inside myself," she whispered. "*Ohh,* now two fingers. In and out. It's warm, slippery and so tight in there."

"I'll get you for this."

A knock at her office door shot Angela up in her seat. *Alice.* Gah! "Yikes, someone at the door, gotta go. When do I get to see you next?"

He chuckled. "Karma in action. I'll be over tonight. Larry got back to me on your pastries, and we should—"

"He did?" She stood and held up her hand at the window to let Alice know she'd be another second. "What's the word?"

"We'll talk about it tonight, okay? You have to go, and I do to."

"Daniel…"

"All hope is not lost. I'll be over after closing. 'Bye."

Honestly. Angela put down the phone. He couldn't just say thumbs up or down? Though maybe there wasn't a final decision yet.

She opened her door. "Sorry, what's up, Alice?"

"Scott needs help out front."

"Sure." She saved the schedule document—lavender

éclairs still on it—and hurried out to the front, where Scott was finishing with one customer and five more waited.

"Who's next?"

Scott jerked his mane of black hair toward a young man, handsome in an unusual way—slightly heavy, dark features, hooded eyes, kind of a sexy Italian cherub.

"Can I help you?"

"Yeah." He was looking at her intently, as if he knew her, while he didn't look at all familiar. "Uh. I'd like to buy some cookies?"

"Sure." She gestured to the trays in the display case. "Any favorites?"

"Not…really."

"An assortment maybe?"

"Oh. Yeah. Okay, yeah."

"How many?"

"Uh…two dozen?"

She nodded and pulled out a box, thinking he was acting like his mom sent him to buy something and he was scared of screwing it up. His mom or maybe a dominatrix girlfriend. *If you do this wrong, Paolo, there's serious punishment happening tonight.* "Two dozen, coming up."

"And cupcakes, too."

"What kind?" She finished packing the cookies and laid them on the counter. "How many?"

"Oh." He frowned, fidgeting uncomfortably. "Two dozen?"

Angela almost giggled. Paolo didn't know how many or what kind. He was getting his bottom paddled for sure. "Assorted flavors?"

"Yeah. Well…make it three dozen. I guess."

He guessed. Maybe the dominatrix girlfriend was having a party, and Paolo got to play serving-boy.

"Any pastries?" She gestured to the international section. "We have an assortment over here that—"

"No, no, I don't want any of those." He spoke as if they

smelled bad. Angela pressed her lips together, making an effort to keep looking pleasant. Not his fault, but she could definitely use a vote of confidence in her recipes right about now. Especially if Slatewood didn't come through. "How about some of those brownies?"

Two dozen cookies, three dozen cupcakes, four dozen assorted brownies, a dozen each scones, muffins and cinnamon rolls later, she was hoping this guy came back often. "That it?"

"That's it." He was still staring at her, and she was pretty sure she didn't look like a dominatrix.

"There you go." Angela handed him the pile of boxes stacked in a paper shopping bag bearing the bakery cornucopia logo. "Come again."

"I'd like to." He backed away a few steps, smiling at her, before he turned and left the shop.

"Someone's crushing on you," Scott murmured next to her.

"Yeah, what was that about?" She smiled welcome at her next customer, her favorite, Marjorie, today dressed in a rich yellow softly tailored suit with matching raincoat, the sunshine Seattle had been irritatingly without this month. "Hi, Marjorie. Ready for your muffin today? Cinnamon roll?"

"I can't live without your cinnamon rolls."

"Cinnamon roll coming up. Did you want to try any pastry today? Another fruit tart?"

"No, thank you, dear." She looked concerned and a bit confused, shaking her head. "If I may say…?"

"Of course." Angela handed her the roll in a waxed bag. "You may say anything."

"Those pastries." She gestured to them with a gaunt ringed hand. "They aren't quite— They lack *passion*."

Angela didn't understand, but this was the second time someone had dissed her international selection in the past ten minutes, and she was not amused. Not today, when Daniel had already declined to talk about the outcome of Slatewood's decision. It felt like a bad omen. "They lack passion?"

"Yes." Marjorie smiled, handing over exact change. "That's it. You're not in love with them. Thank you."

"You're…welcome." Angela looked at her carefully. Were her eyes more vague than usual?

"Hmm." Scott rang up another order as Marjorie walked out. "I think a few brain cylinders misfired there."

"I worry about her."

"You worry about everything. Thanks for saving me. Looks like it's calmed down." He handed the customer staring warily at his earring assortment his change and a receipt. "And one makes five. Thank you, come again."

Angela brushed a grain of chocolate off his shirt and headed for the back. "If you need me again let me know."

"Yo, Angela."

Angela turned around. Jack, holding a folder, looking uncharacteristically animated, came in. "Hey, Jack."

"Got a minute?"

"As a matter of fact, yes." She beckoned to him. "Come on back."

He followed her into her office, greeting a startled Alice with a hug and José with a high five and back slap.

Angela closed the door behind him. "What's going on?"

"I had to show someone. Look at this." He handed her a series of photographs.

Angela studied them. A woman. Long, dark hair, beautiful exotic features. Arms extended, leg lifted, she was dancing. Or doing Tai Chi?

"She's beautiful." More than beautiful. Radiant, with a soulful elegance that was hard to define. Impossible to look at her and not wonder who she was, where she came from, what she was thinking. "Captivating."

"Yes. Yes." He paced Angela's office, which was so small,

the pacing consisted of two steps in either direction. Either he was going to get dizzy or Angela was. "She's perfect."

"Perfect?" She handed the photographs back with a teasing smile. "Are congratulations in order?"

"A perfect model for the new series."

Angela frowned. "This is the girl next door?"

"No. No." Jack stopped pacing, thank goodness, and pushed his hand through his hair. Angela had never seen him this worked up. "I've redefined the whole series. She made me see it in an entirely new way."

"Wow. Jack, this is great." Angela was mystified. Jack hadn't ever shared work stuff with her like this. Unless he was excited about this woman for personal reasons. Which wouldn't be surprising given Jack's history and the woman's looks. "When do you start shooting the series?"

"Oh." He looked uncomfortable. "I haven't approached her with the idea yet."

He hadn't. "Who is she?"

"Uh." He made a face. "I don't know yet."

"Huh?" Angela narrowed her eyes. "Have you actually spoken to this woman?"

"Not exactly."

Angela gaped at him. "My God, I don't think I've ever seen this before. Jack Shea is intimidated by a woman."

"Ha!" He snorted. "Hardly."

"Scares your balls tiny, does she?"

"Angela!" Jack cracked up in earnest, something he let himself do too rarely. "There are few things funnier than coarse language coming out of that sweet mouth of yours."

"You're changing the subject." She handed the photos back to him. "What do you do, hide in the bushes and take pictures of her?"

"I jog through the park every morning. She's there Monday, Wednesday and Friday, 8:00 a.m., like clockwork. This is the first time I had my camera with me." He sat down on the second chair in her office, holding the pictures in his lap, gazing at them. "She defined what I wanted. She made it all clear. Everything about the project I've been waffling on for weeks came to life in a flash. No doubts, no hesitation. That's when you know something is really right."

If that were true, Angela was in trouble. She had doubts and hesitations about pretty much everything. "I'm thrilled for you, Jack.

"All that was missing was seeing how the camera would like her."

"No problems there."

"But now she matters." He laughed self-deprecatingly. "And if I approach her, a complete stranger who, yes, has been taking pictures of her from the bushes, figuratively, anyway, and ask her to model for me…"

Angela winced in sympathy, inwardly loving that mighty Jack was unsure how to handle a female. Probably the first time in his life. "Yeah, the creep factor would be high."

"It's funny, you can be so sure you're on the right path, but sometimes instinct starts telling you you're wrong. If you ignore that voice, you're screwed. If you listen, Fate has a shot at showing you the direction you should have chosen from the beginning." He shook his head, chuckling, face guarded. "I know, don't tell me. I sound like a New Age wacko."

"No, not at all." Well, maybe a little. But his words had disturbed her for another reason.

They sat talking a few minutes longer, Angela trying to help him decide what to do, feeling more and more anxious and upset. She didn't want to hear how a vision could turn out to be completely wrong. She didn't want to hear that Paolo wasn't interested in her pastry or that Marjorie thought it lacked passion.

Daniel was due in two hours; she wanted to hear that her dream was a big piece of chocolate-lavender éclair, already in the bag.

ANGELA HAD JUST emerged from her tiny trickle of a shower when the knock came on her door. Must be one of the gang. Daniel would have to buzz from the front of the building.

"Who's there?"

"Pizza delivery."

She broke into a grin. Daniel after all. Someone must have let him up. Of course she could give him a key to the building, so if he wanted to—

Yikes. Even as the idea gave her romantic side a thrill, her sensible side shut it down in a big hurry. Way too soon for that.

She yanked open the door and got a buzz of pleasure seeing his handsome face, blue eyes the color of the sky not a single Seattle resident had seen all week long, body in jeans and a Rise Against T-shirt, a pizza box balanced on one hand. "Hello, pizza boy. Mmm, hope it's hot and good."

"Well…" His eyes traveled down her towel-covered body. "Something else around here certainly is."

Angela struck a pose. "See anything you like?"

"I think so. But I'll need a closer look." He backed her into her living room, colorful with cookbooks, art prints and bright rugs over hardwood floors, set the pizza on her coffee table and took her into his arms, kissed her deeply, over and over, until she was clinging to him, weak-kneed and breathless. "So far…I like everything."

"Yes?"

"Except this." He unwrapped the towel and let it drop, scanned her body leisurely. "Much better."

"You think?"

He dropped suddenly to his knees, and before she could register what he was doing, his tongue was between her legs, tasting her. The shower had made her skin more sensitive, and the arousal was such that she swayed and grabbed at his shoulder. He responded by gathering her firmly in his arms, head making a lazy circle as he licked her.

"Daniel." Her eyes were practically rolling back in her head.

"Mmm?"

"Bedroom?"

"Later."

She moaned and lowered to give him better access as he slid a finger up inside her, then followed her crevice to the back, where he painted a slow circle in a place she'd never been touched before.

Oh, my. "That is… Oh. Daniel."

"You like that?" he whispered.

"Yes. *Yes.*"

The pressure continued, his mouth explored more boldly, his lips manipulating her clitoris until she felt the climax building, holding her thigh muscles so tight they were trembling. With a sudden furious burst she exploded into orgasm, collapsing over him as the wave swept through her, his strong arms stopping her fall.

He let her come down, one gentle tongue sweep at a time, then kissed her inner thighs, her curls, her abdomen, long lovely farewell kisses, before he stood. And made Angela shriek.

She'd been a limp, ecstatic dishrag draped over him. Now, suddenly she was in a neat fireman's carry, giggling madly on the way to her—

"Bedroom. Now." He made a very respectable caveman. She liked that about him. Especially when he dumped her rather carelessly onto her blue-and-white bedspread, took his clothes off, rolled on a condom at the speed of sound and lunged over her.

Oh, she loved his skin on hers, loved the masculine weight of his body pressing her into the mattress. Her legs opened eagerly under him; she was plenty wet and he slid in easily, dug his arms under her and continued his caveman assault with no pretense at finesse.

Cavemen, as Angela was rapidly finding out, really turned her on. There was something wildly exciting about the force-ful, urgent way Daniel was riding her. She responded au-tomatically, letting out a hoarse cry, bucking against him, determinedly holding onto the last piece of her sanity this time, to keep her from the abyss that had nearly swallowed her at his place.

Daniel thrust a final time, body tight, face contorted in bliss as his climax swept through him. She loved watch-ing this man come; his ecstasy sent an intense sexual thrill through her, almost as if she were climaxing again herself.

"Angela." He was still breathing hard, blue eyes seeming to glow out of his face. "That was…mmm."

"Mmm-*hmm*." She smiled tenderly, lifted her head for an-other long, lovely series of kisses that made the familiar ache start in her chest. Was he feeling it, too?

It didn't matter. Angela would concentrate on staying whole, and staying happy. Right now she was both.

Daniel pulled out, to their simultaneous sounds of regret, disposed of the condom and wrapped strong arms tightly around her, stroking her arm, her hip, making her feel like a cat in the sun. "How was your day?"

"Good. Busy." She yawned and stretched against him. Meo-ow. "The counter went crazy a couple of hours before closing."

She told him about Marjorie and then about Paolo, about his awkward indecision, about his huge order and, giggling, about her dominatrix-girlfriend theory.

Except Daniel didn't seem to be laughing too hard. In fact, he wasn't laughing at all. "That was my roommate."

"Your—" She gaped at him. "But…does he know I'm me?"

"He does."

His grim reaction surprised her. "Daniel, I'm sorry I made fun of him. It wasn't a real insult to him, just a game of—"

"Yeah, I got that. It's fine."

Something still wasn't right. "Why was he staring at me like that? Is he shy?"

"Jake?" Daniel laughed in a way that made it clear shyness was not one of Jake's dominant qualities.

"Then why didn't he introduce himself?"

Daniel swallowed, Adam's apple bobbing. "That's part of what I wanted to talk about today."

Oh. She moved away from him, partly to focus better on his face, and partly because a self-protective instinct told her to, though she kept her hand firmly planted on his chest.

"Larry didn't go for the pastries."

"Ah." She nodded through a quick hot rush of disappointment. "Not entirely unexpected. His niece?"

Daniel looked at her as if he were weighing his next words. "His niece, yes. But I think he also felt…well, what he *said,* was that yours weren't special enough."

Ouch. Not special enough. Lacking in passion. If people wanted to criticize, why couldn't they come up with something concrete so she'd know how to *fix* it?

"What on earth does that mean?"

Daniel sighed. "I think he just didn't care for them."

"Oh." She nodded again. That hurt. She was proud as hell of those recipes. "Well, obviously he doesn't have good taste."

Daniel didn't laugh at her pretend-justification, didn't even smile. He took in a careful breath, obviously feeling the tightrope starting to sway under his feet. "Jake didn't work today. I asked him to come in and buy an assortment of your cookies and cupcakes and so on to bring to Larry instead."

Angela tried to process that, feeling as if her brain had switched into slow motion. "But I told you I didn't need to sell that part of the business. It's going fine. I don't want to expand there."

"I know you did. But I think you have a really good chance

of getting in with the cookies where you couldn't with the pastries."

"Because his niece doesn't make those?"

"Yes, and…" He sighed and turned to face her. "They're incredible. I think they're what you should be doing. I understand that the fancy pastry thing is where your heart lies. Or actually, it's where you think your heart *should* lie. But your true calling, your true passion, is the—"

"Plain, old, ordinary, everyday—"

"Angela." He got up on his elbow, expression earnest, and even in the midst of her recoiling, she felt her heart wanting to reach out to him. "In your hands, they're not ordinary. You have a gift. You elevate cookies and cupcakes and brownies to exactly the level of sophistication and elegance you think you need from pastries."

"*Think* I need?" She pushed herself off the bed.

Daniel sighed. "This isn't going well."

"No, it's not." She started pacing, night table to dresser and back, flung her arm out toward him. "It wasn't your place to decide how I market myself or my bakery."

"No, it wasn't. But if you want in at Slatewood, or more importantly, if you want to make a name for A Taste for All Pleasures, then cookies are the way to go."

She whirled to face him. "Because I'm not quite up to the rest? Because I'm reaching beyond myself and where I belong?"

He ran his hand over his face. "I have to be honest. Yes, I think you are. I think you have this deep need to feel more special, more important, more…whatever it is, I don't even know. Because I can tell you that you are—"

"Not enough."

"*No,* God, no. The opposite. Have you seen how happy your cookies make people?"

"But they don't make *me* happy."

"They should, Angela." He rose to sitting, gloriously rumpled, head turning back and forth to follow her pacing. "Everything about the way you are should make you happy. You don't need to change—"

"So because Larry loved my cookies you want me stuck there forever?"

He sighed. "The irony is that Larry was in a bad mood and wouldn't try them. Said he'd already given you a chance, and they were sticking with Nell. So it was all a big waste of time. Except it's given me the chance to be honest with you."

"Honest, yes." Angela stood, fists clenched, chest heaving to avoid tears. Here it was, the same damn message again. She wasn't good enough to climb higher. She should stay down at the bottom of the pile where she belonged. But this time the announcement came from the one person she thought she could count on to support her, cheer her on, love her not only as she was now, but also as she wanted to be. Now it seemed as if she'd just picked out another Tom.

At least this time she knew her strength, she knew what she wanted in her life and relationships, and what she didn't, what was all-important to her and what was a deal breaker.

Daniel might be the sexiest man she'd ever met, but if he couldn't share her vision for herself, if he was going to keep her down the way Tom had, then he wasn't the man for her.

She opened her mouth to tell him. The words wouldn't come out.

Angela, you have to do this.

For herself, and for her future, she had to have the strength to put herself first when she needed to.

She needed to. Now.

"Daniel…" She turned her face away, unable to look into his eyes. "I think you need to go."

14

BONNIE STARED AT the figures on the printout again. She'd already checked three times for errors, and there were none. The bottom line was worse than she'd expected, and she'd expected bad. Unless business picked up substantially soon, she was in serious trouble.

A wave of nausea made her close her eyes and try to breathe past it. Sweat pricked under her arms. Her vision clouded. She laid her head on the cool top of her desk, trying to calm the anxiety attack.

Of the five Come to Your Senses friends, she'd be the only failure. Angela was doing well enough that she was working to expand. Jack kept himself going shooting weddings and portraits so he could concentrate on the art photography he loved best. Demi seemed to have a steady stream of clients. Seth had inherited enough money to buy a small country, so he had the luxury of working at what he loved, regardless of income.

Bonnie had no such luxury. She'd used money inherited from her grandmother to open Bonnie Blooms, and now she was on her own. Her parents hadn't understood or supported her dream of owning her own shop. Conventional to the point of tedium, Mom and Dad believed any possible risk should be avoided. Leaving the house without an umbrella on a cloudy day? Why on earth would anyone take a chance like that? Bonnie was up against that attitude when she announced her plans to start a business not only by spending a good chunk of her savings, but also by taking on a load of debt only years of decent profits would erase.

Needless to say, they had not been enthusiastic. Now, a year later, Bonnie had yet to make anything close to decent profits.

New businesses took a while to get going. She knew that, and had been prepared, she thought. But she'd bet every outwardly sensible entrepreneur dove in secretly convinced the world would be changed by what he or she offered. Bonnie had been the same. Look at her shop. It was gorgeous. How could anyone *not* want flowers this beautiful, this tempting, this reasonably priced?

Apparently they could. So she was faced with the grim prospect of coming up with a way to get herself noticed or continuing to deplete her savings until she had to cry uncle.

The bad news? As if that wasn't enough? Marketing was not her strong suit. Her creative strength was visual, not words or concepts. Others at Come to Your Senses were more talented in that area, but to enlist their help, she'd have to admit she was struggling. Her pride hadn't allowed that yet. She'd always been fiercely independent, probably to a fault, and she still clung to the hope that she could dig herself out of this alone.

What if she couldn't?

The nausea swept her again. *Deep breaths. Positive thoughts.*

Everything was going to be okay. She was young, strong, smart and she was going to be fine. There were more ways she could economize before she had to give up, including subletting her apartment and moving into the shop's office. She wouldn't be able to hide that from the others, but she could make something up about a friend who needed a place to stay, and Bonnie didn't mind a downstairs cot.

Yeah, she wouldn't buy it, either.

Tears came. She was so tired. Too tired to fight them, too tired to go upstairs so she could bawl in private. She wasn't sleeping, was losing weight from not eating well or enough. That had to change. She couldn't get sick. Hiring someone to run the store while she was out of commission would put her back further than fresh meat, fruits and vegetables once in a while. Once a week? Twice? Could she manage that?

She didn't know. She was too tired to figure it out.

The building's front entrance opened. Bonnie reached hastily to turned out the lamp at her desk so she wouldn't be seen. Someone coming back from a Saturday night out? Footsteps sounded out in the hall, pausing by her door. She hadn't bothered locking the shop since the building was closed for the night.

Go away, whoever you are.

No such luck. Footsteps sounded in among her flowers.

"Hey. What are you doing up so late, little girl?"

Seth, heading for her office. Where had he been? Out doing something not-sexual again with the sexiest woman in Seattle?

"Working." She tried to sound cheerful, quickly took the disastrous budget report off the screen and kept her gaze on the monitor so he wouldn't see her tears.

"All work and no play…"

"You play enough for both of us." That actually wasn't true, he worked like a demon possessed, composing, teaching, getting the word out about his music, trying always to find new avenues for its performance, but right now attack was her only defense.

"Yes, ma'am." He drew up a chair behind her, in the corner of her office where she'd imagined a cot could go if she moved some file cabinets. In her peripheral vision she saw him cross his long, strong legs and fold his arms. As if he were going to stay awhile, damn it. "How's business?"

"Fine. Great." She couldn't manage more on that topic. "How's your film director?"

"Still waffling. I probably won't hear for a few weeks still."

"Look…" She rubbed her eyes. "I'm pretty busy right now, Seth. Would you mind leaving me alone?"

"Yes. I would."

Her body stiffened. She turned her head for emphasis, giving him her profile. "I need you to leave."

"I need to stay."

"Why?"

"Because my sweet, darling Bonnie, you've been crying, and that freaks me out because you never do." He leaned forward, resting his arms on his thighs. "Except because of me, which I could never fix. But I don't think this is about me, and I am going to stay like a wart on a log until you tell me what it is, so I can help you."

"Logs don't have warts, they have bumps."

"This log has warts. Nasty ones. With hair."

She managed a brief snort of laughter. He had the sense of humor of a twelve-year-old boy, but having grown up with brothers, she did, too. "Moles have hair, not warts."

"Are you going to keep deflecting the subject with your know-it-all corrections or talk to me?"

"The first one."

"Fine." He got to his feet. "This calls for serious action."

Familiar enjoyable alarm shot through her. You never knew with Seth. "What are you going to do?"

"This is for your own good." He took the keyboard off her lap, pulled her to her feet. "I advise you not to resist."

"Jeez." She tried to pull away. "What are you going to do, spank me?"

"Mmm, Bonnie, do *not* tempt me like that."

She blushed crimson, knowing exactly the night and place they were both flashing back to. Sex with Seth had been unlike anything she'd ever known. Things bodies could do together, to each other, that would ordinarily have horrified her, had been highly erotic with him. She'd never met anyone so uninhibited, no one who'd been able to get at the dark sexual side of herself she hadn't known existed.

"Seriously, Seth. I have work to do. Whatever you're planning, you can just—"

"Shh. Relax." He pulled her out of the office, pulled her stiff body toward him, right hand at her waist, left hand holding hers. "I'm just going to dance with you."

He was going to dance with her? Of all the ridiculous—

His light baritone filled the shop and her senses with "Summer Wind," the song many sang, but in Seth's eyes Frank Sinatra owned. He danced her gently around flowers, some at eye level, some waist, some knee, her beautiful English garden.

Bonnie sighed. He smelled so, so good. Like Seth. And he felt good. And she so needed arms around her right now. Even chaste ones. Even Seth's.

She gave in, relaxed against him and let herself be danced. He pulled her closer, right arm circling her waist, chin at her temple, her left hand brought in to rest on his shoulder. His chest was warm and solid under her cheek; she could hear and feel his voice rumbling through it.

Tears came again in a steady silent stream she couldn't stop and prayed he wouldn't notice. It was all too much. The shaky finances of her store, being in Seth's arms again, and a song about love and loss.

"Hey, Bon-bon."

"Mmm?" The syllable was all she could manage.

"Remember that time your birth control messed up and you were pregnant by that guy you were seeing? What was his name...Roger?"

The beautiful spell snapped like a twig. God, why was he bringing *that* up. Roger had dumped her a week before her period was late, and she'd been a mess. Seth, only a friend then, had found her crying and was so sweet Bonnie had spilled out her pain and her fear. He'd gone with her to the drugstore, held her hand while they waited for the test results, went with her to the doctor and stood by her during the unexpected miscarriage two weeks later. Not long after that they were a couple, then and for the next wonderful year until he panicked.

"I was the only person you told. Is that still true?"

She nodded against his chest.

"Remember you asked me never to tell anyone?"

She nodded again.

"I never did, Bonnie."

"Why are you talking about this now?"

He stopped dancing, put her arms around his neck, put both of his around her and gazed down at her, his handsome face more serious than she'd seen it in years. "I know I've screwed up big-time with you. I know I hurt you badly. I know that there are still feelings between us, and that you are frustrated sometimes."

"Seth, don't, not now, I can't—"

"Shh, please." His finger landed gently on her lips. "Just let me tell you two things. One, I'm frustrated, too. You are still the most amazing, funny, sexy, fabulous woman I've ever met."

Bonnie swallowed more tears. He undoubtedly thought he was being sweet, but he might as well stick a rusty knife through her stomach. Far kinder to tell her she had no hope of ever being with him again. "What's the second thing?"

"I'm still a guy you can tell anything to, Bonnie. And you'd still be completely safe doing it."

She stood in his arms, staring at his chest. Outside it had begun to rain; drops pelted her windows, making it feel warmer and more intimate inside, fresh with the smell of her beloved flowers. And she made her decision, too exhausted and burdened to care if it was a good one or not.

"The store is not doing well."

He stiffened. She lifted her head to look at him. Familiar as his features were, they still startled her sometimes with their beauty. In the dim light of the shop they did so now. Strong square jaw she used to tease him he borrowed from Ashton Kutcher; high forehead under spiked brown hair; narrow hazel eyes that made him look gang-member fierce unless he was laughing. His mouth, surrounded by faint gray stubble on flawless skin, was a work of art. He'd had several offers to model from age sixteen on, all of which he'd turned down.

"How bad?" He could have been asking about the weather, which made it easier for her to continue.

"I'm thinking about moving into the office."

"God, Bonnie." His hands gripped her shoulders. "Why didn't you tell me? I have plenty of money. I could—"

"No." Her chin went up. "I'm not taking your money. That's not why I'm telling you this."

"Of course not." He looked away and back, clearly upset. "But it's just sitting there doing me no good. Why won't you let me help you?"

She couldn't explain. He didn't understand what it was like when money really mattered: having, not having, borrowing, buying, spending, owing. All of it was a game to him. No stakes at all. "I can't. It's too…"

Intimate. Another reason. Seth riding in again for Bonnie's rescue. She couldn't handle that emotionally.

"Well, for God's sake, Bonnie, if you're moving anywhere it's in with me."

She snorted. "Oh, *there's* a good idea."

"No, okay, not a good idea. But…" He took a deep breath. "Okay, how about this. How do *you* want me to help?"

Her eyebrows rose. What did *she* want? Well. That was new.

"I guess just listen. Sprinkle me with a little sympathy now and then. Make sure I'm never alone, even for a second. Keep replenishing my supply of mood-altering drugs." She forced a teasing smile. "I really don't know, Seth. I'm just starting to face this myself. I need more people in the shop every day, and I need to sign on more repeat customers, weekly orders for hotel and office lobbies, that kind of stuff. The problem is that the established businesses already have florists, most of whom are also established and therefore can price lower than I can. And there aren't a whole lot of new businesses popping up these days."

"You need to get the word out somehow." He frowned. "Will you let me do some thinking about this?"

"Sure." Unexpected relief flooded her, even though nothing had been solved. "Thank you, Seth."

"Newsflash for you." He brought her back close, still holding her shoulders. "It is al-ways o-*kay* to ask for help."

He was joking now, enunciating like a grade-school reading teacher, but still Bonnie caught her breath. When he was like this, tender and caring, when he made it clear how well he still knew her, understood her, and wanted to be there for her, she was in the most danger.

"What is this thing called 'ask for help'? Is that what they do on your planet?"

"Yes." He slid his hands down her arms, took her fingers in his. "And more than that, it is particularly okay to ask *me* for help."

"I'll *try* to remember…"

He moved back then forward, extending and contracting their arms, a slow jitterbug step. "I hate that you've been going through this crap by yourself. You don't need to do that. You don't *ever* need to do that. You can always come to me. Promise?"

She nodded demurely, hiding how he moved her. "Yes, Daddy, I promise."

He chuckled and lifted their clasped hands to one side and over their heads, locking them together. "Okay, wise-ass, *now* I'm going to spank you."

"Are you promising, too?" She batted her eyes, giddy at having someone to confide in. No, giddy at having *Seth* to confide in, even if he was the last person she should turn to. Look what sharing her secret burden had accomplished in college? She and Seth had been alone in the private world of her tragedy, an intimate world that had bonded them, eventually into love.

Well…she'd called it love; Seth never made it half that far.

He turned them in a slow circle, locking his eyes on hers.

Bonnie would have to be on extra double guard to make sure that didn't happen again. She didn't think she could survive finding and losing him a second time.

"So…" Seth lifted their arms back to neutral, continued the slow jitterbug. "Now that we've solved all your problems, what do you think about coming up to my place for a celebratory drink?"

"Said the spider to the fly."

"C'mon, Bonnie, I'm not going to hit on you when you're miserable and vulnerable."

"No?"

"No. Absolutely not." He shook his head emphatically. "I'll cheer you up, then I'll hit on you."

"Oh, *that's* comforting." Bonnie dropped his hands and pushed him away, hiding laughter.

"I'll behave like a Boy Scout. No, a eunuch." He moved toward her front door and held out his hand. "No risk, just a friendly drink."

He continued to extend his hand. "Come with me?"

Bonnie hesitated. He'd been right that she was miserable and vulnerable, and here he was, Prince Charming, offering to lead her up the steps to his castle on feet of clay. Offering to pour her a magic potion he promised would make everything better.

If she were reading this fairy tale, she'd be yelling at the heroine not to be an idiot, to run, fast and far, shack up with the first dwarf or beast or ogre she found. Anyone but this guy.

On the other hand, Seth had promised to be a gentleman. Bonnie did trust him that far. And the alternative was going back to her cold, empty apartment to listen to the rain and think about how she might not be able to afford the place for long.

She took his hand. "One drink. Maybe we can brainstorm some ideas for—"

"Not tonight. You won't starve this week, I won't let you. And you need some fun in your life right now, a break from responsibility. I want to do that for you, just for a few days."

"Hey." She pulled her hand away. "This started with one drink. Now you're taking me over for a few days?"

"And then the brainwashing begins." He did a credible impression of a movie villain's laugh. "Soon you will be completely in my power."

"Oh, please." Bonnie glared in disdain, thinking brainwashing would be way too little, way too late. She might as well admit she was already in Seth's power, had been since the first time he kissed her, six years earlier.

And despite what she'd told herself and everyone else about her feelings and her future, she might as well admit right now that she probably always would be.

15

"WHOA. WHO dressed you this morning?" Daniel held a carton of milk over his coffee, ready to pour.

"Like it?" Jake modeled his skinny vest, tie and shirt combination.

"You look sharp. Completely different." He acknowledged Jake's glare with a grin. "What's the occasion?"

"I met a girl. A woman, actually."

"A *woman*. Well." Daniel put his hands on his hips, regarding his roommate with amusement. This sounded as serious as Jake looked. "Is that where you've been every night recently?"

"Yup." He poured himself orange juice and gulped it.

"Why have you been coming home every night?"

"We haven't gotten to that."

Daniel's eyebrow shot up. When Jake "met" a woman, it meant he'd spent the night with her. "You're slipping."

He rubbed his finger absently over a splash of juice on the counter. "She's different. Special. I have this feeling about her, I don't know."

"Yeah?" Daniel knew. He'd had a feeling about Angela the second he'd laid eyes on her. And because of her he'd been awake too much of the previous three nights, about as miserable as he'd been the first time walking into her bakery to buy cupcakes for Kate's birthday. Seemed a lifetime ago. Given his rebirth since he met Angela, it nearly was. "Where are you going tonight?"

"She hangs at the Purple Café on Tuesdays."

"Classy woman then." He put the milk back into the refrigerator.

"Very." Jake poured himself a cup of coffee looking more nervous than Daniel had ever seen him. "Probably too classy for me. I'm not sure how to handle this. I talk to her, we have a good time, but she won't go out with me."

"Wait…what?" Daniel put down his mug without taking a sip. "You've seen her practically every night and none of them have been dates? What are you doing, stalking her around the city?"

"Uhhh…" He shrugged, tugging at his tie. "Pretty much."

Daniel was flabbergasted. "This strikes you as a good idea?"

"She's going to cave. I feel it. I know it. And as long as I feel that, I'm not giving up until she says yes. Even if I have to be pathetic."

Daniel had no idea what to say to that. The idea that Jake would crawl to a woman… He didn't know whether to offer congratulations or sympathy.

"I have to go, man. Early meeting." Jake held his fist up for a bump.

"Yeah. Okay. Good luck tonight." Shaking his head, Daniel took his coffee into his bedroom, where he'd laid out his clothes. Jake caught, finally, by a woman who didn't want him.

Unfortunately at this moment, Daniel knew how that felt.

He turned away from his new wall decoration, bought with Angela's teasing about his colorless room in mind. The vintage poster showed automaker Peugot's lion mascot holding a bicycle in his mouth. Reddish orange, blue, yellow...Angela gave the place even more color, just by walking into it.

Daniel sighed and started dressing for work. He'd screwed up by not talking to Angela about passing along her cookies to Larry. He'd just felt so strongly those were her best shot, and he'd wanted to surprise her with the success she dreamed about, even if it wasn't exactly in the form she originally planned. Life changed. Dreams changed. You rolled with the punches or stood still and got a serious shiner. You lost beautiful Kate and while stumbling along the brutal path away from her, found Angela. You struck out with éclairs and tried cupcakes.

He should have been tougher when Larry childishly refused to try the second batch of samples. But his boss had been in a foul mood— "Haven't we been through this? Didn't I give you an answer already? She doesn't cut it." He was not swayed by Daniel's assertion that this was a different level of baking altogether. "You'll have to impress your girlfriend some other way."

So Daniel, with a solid chance to be Angela's knight in shining armor, at the first sign of trouble, had turned tail and run. Look at Jake still going after this woman every night with no success in sight.

Coffee cup rinsed in the kitchen, he went into the bathroom to brush his teeth. Jake wasn't giving up. Kate wouldn't have given up. And she wouldn't have let Daniel give up, either.

He wasn't going to. Angela had brought him out of grief and into new strength. In return, he wasn't going to sit back and let her sabotage herself by thinking she wasn't good enough to be special, by thinking her ex and his snotty family had been right about her all along. She was incredibly special, and if Daniel couldn't prove that to her, then he didn't deserve to have her in his life.

Teeth brushed, he went into the kitchen and loaded up the

goodies Jake had bought the week before, kept in his freezer, enough for an army of Larrys, and headed downstairs for his car.

At work, he went straight to the break room, laid out the cookies, cupcakes, brownies, cinnamon rolls, scones and muffins, after refreshing them in the microwave, on platters he found in underneath cabinets. Then he went back to his desk and waited.

Not long. Within the hour there was a steady stream in and out of the break room as word spread to other departments. Moans of ecstasy, exclamations of bliss. *Oh, my god. These are so-o-o good.* And over and over again, *Who brought these? Where are they from? How can we get more?*

Grinning like a smug crocodile, Daniel got to his feet and went out into the main office area. Nearly every desk had a cookie, muffin, cinnamon roll or scone on it. A few people still lingered in the break room, loading up on seconds.

As if summoned by the sugar gods, Larry came out of his office, staring intently at a sheaf of papers. He looked up. Frowned. Gazed around the office, which gradually quieted. "What the hell is going on? Whose birthday? Why wasn't I told?"

Chuckling, Daniel swiped an enormous chocolate-chunk macadamia from Rebecca's desk and brought it over to his boss.

"Here you go, Larry. Have a cookie on me."

"CAN I HELP YOU?" Angela forced a smile at the middle-aged woman at her counter, feeling as if she'd been put through a washing machine. Agitated, spun in circles, nearly drowned. She'd hardly slept all weekend, going over the argument with Daniel, sometimes furious that he'd betrayed her, sometimes wondering what she wasn't seeing, what part of this was her fault, how she could have misinterpreted the crisis. Because he was so…not like Tom.

The customer ordered a box of assorted pastries, to take home for dinner. In a stroke of bitter irony, the éclairs and fruit tarts had been selling well that day. What was that supposed to mean? That Daniel was wrong? That there was plenty of passion left in her passion-fruit mousse cake? She wished she had a more objective way of telling.

The customer paid and left the shop, which stayed empty behind her, as it often did after lunch, before students started coming in for afternoon snacks followed by the post-work crowd buying breads for dinner or breakfast items for the following morning.

Angela sighed and wiped down the counter, got out glass cleaner and started in on the smudges that exploring little fingers and careless big ones had left on her cases. She was supposed to give the lemon-rosemary Madeleine recipe another go today, but she couldn't summon much energy or enthusiasm.

All she wanted was to have Daniel back the way things were before last Friday, they way he was when he embodied all her fantasies of what a relationship could be.

But she supposed that was juvenile. The odds of finding her perfect match on the first try after her divorce were minuscule. And no one was going to be perfect anyway. Or if there was a perfect match out there somewhere, chances were he was already married, or lived in the mountains of North Carolina or the swamps of Florida or the shores of Tripoli, and she'd never, ever find him.

Daniel had a right to his opinion, and he had every right to tell her that opinion as well. But she also had a right, which was to be with someone who'd share her vision as well as her body. Next time, with the next guy, she wasn't going to hop into his bed until she was sure of him, of them, of the type of man he was. She'd learned that lesson well.

The next guy. God, she couldn't stand thinking about it. Or him. In fact, she didn't even like him. Even in the short time she'd known Daniel, he'd crept into her fantasies about the future. There wasn't room for this other guy. He was horrible in comparison. He smelled bad. He picked his teeth at dinner.

He wasn't Daniel.

She was doomed. Doomed to moon over a man who wasn't right for her for the rest of her life.

"Hey." In another sickening coincidence, at that moment Bonnie, lifelong mooner after a man not right for her, dragged herself into the bakery, looking particularly pale and thin, especially since she was wearing black jeans and a gray shirt, nothing like her customary colorful plumage. Even her hair looked tired. "I need fat and sugar."

"I agree." Angela went back behind the counter. "You're not eating enough and you look miserable. Here."

"Thanks." Bonnie took the small stack of walnut chocolate-chunk cookies and slumped onto a stool by the counter where Angela's pots of coffee stood.

"You going to tell me what's wrong?"

"You go first. I might look miserable, but you look like hell."

"Why thank you." Angela grimaced, not even able to laugh at the joke. "Man trouble. You?"

"Man trouble." She took a big bite of cookie.

"Seth?"

"Seth." She pointed to Angela. "Daniel?"

Angela sighed. "Daniel."

"Why do we do this to ourselves?"

"I don't know. So the species survives?"

"Not with the sex I'm getting. Or rather not getting."

"That's actually good." Angela retrieved her cleaner and rag and put them behind the counter. "If you were sleeping with him you'd get your heart smashed even worse."

"I know. But at least I'd be getting laid." She sighed nearly as long and painfully as Angela had. "What did Daniel do?"

"Hi, ladies." Scott strode in, ready to start his working day, his metal-ware sparkling, black hair freshly combed. "What's going on?"

"Oh. Nothing. Hi, Scott." Angela made a stab at smiling.

"We're plotting the eradication of your gender." Bonnie glared at him maniacally. "One odious specimen at a time."

"Ah…" Scott backed toward the kitchen. "I'll, um, just get out of your way, then."

Bonnie grinned in satisfaction as he disappeared. "Nothing like a little hate to brighten up your day."

"Nice, Bonnie. He's probably climbing out a window and we'll never see him again."

"He'll be back." She slumped onto the counter, letting her head loll onto her arm. "Tell me what Daniel is doing. Or not doing."

"Not doing. He isn't—" Angela's cell rang; she forwarded bakery calls while she was alone in the store, so she wouldn't have to run back to her office. "Hang on. I need to get this. Hello, A Taste of All Pleasures, this is Angela speaking."

"Angela, this is Tracy Baguerra, Larry Kaiser's secretary over at Slatewood International."

"Slatewood. Yes, of course, hello." She opened her eyes wide at Bonnie, who opened hers even wider back. "How can I help you?"

"Larry would like to hire you for our Spring Fling party, on May twenty-eighth."

"Oh, wonderful. Thank you, very much." She flashed a thumbs up at Bonnie, spirits rising halfway to normal for the first time in days. Slatewood wanted her after all. Had Larry's niece gotten another gig? Wow. Angela's new line would finally be getting air time. "Do you need more of my pastry samples for—"

"Sorry, I wasn't clear. His niece does the pastry for us."

"Ah." Angela's smile clouded. Across the room so did Bonnie's. "Then what do you need from me?"

She guessed the answer before it came.

"We need to cut our costs this year, so we'd like to serve cookies alongside the pastries, maybe some of those cinnamon rolls, if you can make them smaller. We'll have about two hundred people."

They wanted cookies. Because cookies were cheap. Larry hadn't tried hers, why bother? Anyone could make them.

"Of course." She wanted to hang up the phone. She wanted to tell the woman to go to hell and hang up the phone. But of course that was silly. Business was business and she was in no position to spit on a company like Slatewood. Daniel was probably right. This was better than nothing. "That is great, thank you."

"If you could email us a list of available options and pricing that would be very helpful."

"Yes. Right away. I will." She wrote down the woman's name and address and hung up the phone. "Well…"

"I couldn't tell, was that good news or bad?"

"I can't tell, either, Bonnie." She put her hands to her hot cheeks. "I'm so confused right now."

"You're in good company at least." She took another mournful bite of cookie. "What are you confused about, specifically?"

"Slatewood wants the boss's niece for pastry, me for cookies. I feel as if I'm the only person excited about my new line. Marjorie's not, Tom's not, Daniel's definitely not, and now Slatewood isn't, either."

Bonnie frowned, pressing her lips together. "Have you tasted the pastry this niece makes?"

"No." She brightened. That could help.

"We're going." Bonnie pointed to Angela's kitchen. "Tell Scott to mind the store. We'll ingest some serious calories, and see what the fuss is about. Maybe that will give you some answers."

Ten minutes later, they'd climbed into Bonnie's Ford Fiesta

and were on their way to Nell's bakery on 4th Avenue, a few blocks from the water, Angela nervous as hell. She couldn't help feeling as if coming face-to-face with this woman's pastries would be a self-defining moment.

If only she could get rid of the certainty she'd end up having to define herself as a failure.

Nell's was located on the ground floor of the Greymont Hotel, a white stone building flying colorful flags. The bakery storefront was mostly glass, its beautiful logo centered in gold on either side of the door. Inside, white round tables with black iron chairs set a continental look. Behind, gleaming cases of glass and gold held row upon row of colorful, perfect pastries, cakes, rolls, cookies and breads, each neatly lined, each with a silver holder and laminated tag naming and describing the item. Triangular lemon mousse cakes decorated with tiny matching macaroons, pistachio *bûches de Noël*, glistening with chocolate, growing perfect marzipan mushrooms dusted with cocoa powder. Napoleons, croissants, brioche with shining topknots, all presented in a variety of flavors. Petits fours topped with delicate chocolate cutouts, fruit tarts shining with jelly glaze, éclairs in a variety of sizes, some with what looked like gold dust scattered over the chocolate topping.

Truly extravagant. Truly special.

The two women behind the counter, one blond, one brunette, were smiling and friendly, and so exotically beautiful, with such poise, they could have been actresses or models. Their elegant presence lent the shop an even more exclusive atmosphere.

Exactly the type of bakery Angela had always wanted.

She and Bonnie waited in line, Angela getting more and more miserable as customers exclaimed over their purchases and sighed wistfully over choices they were forced to make, leaving other dainties untasted.

"Can I help you?" The dark woman, smiling at Bonnie, had a throaty French accent. Of course.

"She's buying." Bonnie gestured to Angela. "She has her own bakery, A Taste for All Pleasures. We're here to check out the competition."

Angel groaned. *Bonnie…*

The woman's face lit up. "Yes, I know where you are. My sister has found your place. She says your cinnamon rolls changed her life."

"Thank you." Angela forced a smile. "That's nice to hear."

"What can I get you today, ladies?"

"I'll have a chocolate-raspberry croissant," Bonnie announced. "Angela?"

"An apricot hazelnut napoleon." Apricots. Hazelnuts. Brilliant.

"Certainly." The woman rang up the pastries with graceful efficiency and wished them a warm *bon appetit*.

While she poured wonderful-smelling coffee from the pots on the counter into porcelain mugs instead of the thick paper cups she provided, Angela tried to imagine teaching Scott to say *bon appetit*. And failed.

She and Bonnie sat at a spotless table and stared apprehensively at the croissant, the napoleon and each other.

"Okay. Here goes." Bonnie picked up her croissant, opened her mouth and sank in her teeth. The crust crackled audibly; her eyes went wide, then, as she started to chew, closed in rapture.

Courage, Angela.

Her fork went easily into the napoleon, which could be tough if the pastry wasn't perfectly fresh and perfectly baked. The forkful went just as easily into her mouth.

Ohh. Intensely flavored apricot, enriched with a pastry cream so light and clear-tasting she didn't feel a single calorie. The hazelnuts added a pleasant crunch and their strong flavor stayed in perfect balance to the whole.

A few more bites eaten in reverent silence, then she and Bonnie switched plates to try each other's bit of heaven. Angela picked up the croissant. The crust shattered into buttery flakes; the inside was warm, moist and slightly chewy, with tangy raspberry flavor from fresh berries, not jam, mingled with rich dark chocolate.

Every flavor was distinct, clean and of top quality. Every texture was ethereal, on its own and in combination. Simply put, Nell was a genius, next to whom Angela was an amateur. Marjorie's comment made sudden and glaring sense. These pastries were all about passion. No matter how hard and how meticulously Angela worked on her recipes she couldn't come close to this.

"Excuse me." A woman in a gold-and-white striped apron lightly dusted with flour stood beside their table. "Which of you owns A Taste for All Pleasures?"

"That's me." Angela nodded, horrified by a sudden urge to cry. This would, of course, be the genius herself. All this time Angela had worked her ass off, hungering for what Nell did, thinking she was getting close, and now she realized for the first time, how far away she was. Too far ever to catch up. "I'm Angela Loukas."

"Nell Kaiser. So nice to meet you. I guess we'll be sharing the stage at Slatewood this spring? My uncle mentioned you." She leaned forward confidentially. "He said I better have a taste of your cookies. That I might learn something."

"Ha!" As if. "I doubt that."

"You *should* try her cookies." Bonnie rummaged under the table and triumphantly produced a small pastry box with Angela's logo on it, which she opened and offered to Nell. "How about now?"

"Bonnie." Angela's face caught fire. When had Bonnie put the box together? Angela did not need this humiliation. This was like handing Picasso your finger-painting project. Like sending Einstein your arithmetic homework. Like—

"Oh. My. God." Nell was chewing. She turned to Angela, genuine awe in her eyes. "There are absolutely incredible."

Angela blinked. Blinked again. Say what?

A sharp pain in her shin made her jump. Bonnie had kicked her.

"I'm glad you like them." Her voice shook. Was this really happening?

"The texture." Nell took another bite, frowning, concentrating. "Some really cool combination of sugars? What temperature do you bake these at? Low-protein flour? You must use chocolate from—" She broke off laughing. "Listen to me, trying to get your secrets. Man, these make me want to take my own cookies off the shelves and hide in shame."

Angela gaped. Gaped some more until she got another pain in her shin. "Thank you. Really. I was thinking a minute ago I'd pledge my firstborn child for your way with napoleons."

Nell nodded, not pridefully, but looking perplexed. "It's funny, isn't it. Some recipes respond to us better than others. And it's not always the ones you love the most."

"No?" Angela shook herself, not wanting to appear clueless. "I mean no. Absolutely. What do you love most?"

"Cupcakes!" She gestured into the air and let her hand drop. "I really wanted to open a cupcake shop. I worked my butt off, tried every variation of every recipe I could think of, but in the end I was defeated."

"Angela's cupcakes are *to die for.*" Bonnie grinned loyally.

"Trust me, I've heard. Uncle Larry will probably ask for hourly deliveries the way he was talking." She spoke without a trace of jealousy. "But cupcakes and I aren't a good match. It's like dating. You might be crazy about some guy, but if he couldn't care less about you…"

"Éclairs don't love me." Angela gave a hiccup of laughter, suddenly and ridiculously giddy. "Neither do fruit tarts or petits fours. Madeleines outright wish I was dead."

Nell laughed and gestured to the cases. "You're looking only at the pastries I fit with. These recipes and I belong together. You can't fight that."

Angela nodded, yes, yes, yes. She'd been told this before. By Tom, by Marjorie, by Jack, by Bonnie, bless her heart, and by Daniel. But how much more lovely to think that cookies loved her or that she and cupcakes belonged together, than to think she wasn't good enough for anything else.

She had been reaching beyond herself. Her mistake was in assuming that she was reaching for something better and of more value.

"Thank you for coming out to say hello." She stood and shook Nell's hand warmly in both of hers. "I can't thank you enough for the compliments. I've been having something of a crisis of confidence lately."

"Ha!" Nell nodded sympathetically. "I live in crises of confidence. I finally decided when you stop having crises, you've stopped caring, and it's time to retire and do something else."

Angela laughed, light as air in spite of the quantities of fat and sugar she'd just consumed. "It has been really, really nice meeting you."

"Same here. I'm looking forward to working with you. We're going to throw a hell of a party together." She looked longingly at the box on the table in front of Bonnie. "Can I...?"

"Absolutely." Angela took the box and handed it to Nell, wanting to hug her. And then hug Bonnie for believing in her enough to bring it along.

And then wanting to rush back to A Taste for All Pleasures and tell Scott to stay until closing because she was going to find another person who'd believed in her enough to recognize her true talent and send it over to a boss who'd already said no. A man she belonged with as much as if not more than she belonged with her cupcakes and cookies, cinnamon rolls and muffins.

A man she truly loved.

16

"Scott, I need you to take over for an hour or so, okay?" Angela practically skidded to a stop at her front counter. No customers. Good. She'd feel less guilty. "You can call Alice out if things get tough."

"Sure, no problem." His too-black brows furrowed. "Everything okay?"

"Yes! Fine!" Everything was more than okay. Everything was wonderful, amazing, perfect and fan-freaking-tastic. Or would be as soon as Daniel forgave her. Which he would, wouldn't he? Of course he would. Because the alternative was unthinkable. "Why do you ask?"

"You seem a little flustered."

"Do I?" She put a hand to her burning cheeks and laughed like a village idiot. "Well, no. I mean maybe a little, but nothing bad has happened. I just need time to…straighten something out."

He held up his hand as if he were taking an oath. "You can count on me."

"I do." She smiled. Scott was wonderful. Alice would be in soon, she was wonderful. It was April twenty-ninth, still in the fifties and raining, and *that* was wonderful, too.

Daniel had believed in her. More than she'd believed in herself.

Sudden inspiration hit. "Be right back."

She dashed into the kitchen, grabbed a chocolate-chocolate cupcake and packed it in one of the fancy small boxes she'd invested in recently, perfect for thinking-of-you gifts. Or I-love-you gifts, like this one.

"Back in a bit." She flew to the bakery door, then remembered she'd driven to Nell's bakery with Bonnie, and didn't have her car keys. "Oh, wait."

Whirling, she ran back to her office, grabbed the keys and left again, calling another goodbye to Scott.

Three steps from the building's front door, she remembered her umbrella. Not a good idea to show up at Daniel's apartment looking like a drowned rat.

Back into her office, past a visibly amused Scott, not that she blamed him, she grabbed her umbrella and rushed back into the store. "So, um, Scott."

"Don't tell me. Let me guess. You're leaving now?"

"Well." She sighed. "That's sort of been the plan all along."

He grinned. "Good luck with whatever it is, Angela. I'm behind you."

"Thank you, Scott. Thank you." She nearly teared up. The kid deserved a raise. She'd give him one when she got back. She'd give everyone raises. And champagne! They deserved it. A Taste for All Pleasures was in at Slatewood! If that went well and the word spread, she'd be on her way to less worry and higher profits. Those were good things. Even without the trappings she'd dreamed of.

Into her car, tossing the umbrella onto the seat next to her, out onto Broadway, heading for Slatewood's offices on 5th Avenue South. She was on her way.

Except she wasn't. The traffic slowed to a crawl. What should be a five-minute drive would take longer.

A lot longer.

She glanced at her watch. Four-thirty. At least she'd make it by five before Daniel left for the day.

Four-fifty-five, after having to park at the far end of the huge lot behind the Slatewood headquarters, she was in the reception area, breathless from running.

"I'd like to see Daniel Flynn, please."

DANIEL TOOK the pan of chocolate cupcakes out of the oven and sniffed. Hmm. They smelled okay. Sort of. They looked funny. The tops weren't gently rounded, but had spread flat over the pan, and their edges looked charred. Maybe he'd overfilled them? The recipe had said two-thirds full, but that hadn't seemed like enough.

Apparently it was.

He'd cut the recipe down to make six cupcakes, because he only needed one. Maybe the recipe hadn't liked being divided? Too late now. He looked the mess over critically. If he trimmed one and covered it liberally with frosting, he'd be okay. It was the thought that counted, right? Angela wouldn't expect perfect baking from him.

Though, uh, he wasn't that sure about the frosting. He didn't have a sifter, so he'd measured the confectioner's sugar as is. He figured the mixer would take care of the lumps, and it had. Sort of. Unfortunately, when he added the sugar and cocoa to the butter with the mixer running on high, brown and white powder had flown all over the counter and floor and him. Then the mixture had seemed too thin, so he'd dumped in more sugar, which made it too thick, so he'd added more milk as the recipe suggested, only it turned out to be too much. More cocoa, too much, a tiny splash of milk…that had fixed it. He thought.

A glance at his watch told him this process had gone on way too long. He'd wanted to catch Angela after Scott showed up for work, so Scott could take over the counter while he talked to her, but before she got busy with closing up duties.

It was just after five now. He'd left work at two, after a meeting he couldn't miss, and had rushed to do his errands, knowing if he ran into trouble with his first purchase he'd be cutting it close making cupcakes afterward.

He had. He was.

Now, to save time, he'd have to frost the cupcakes before they cooled. He chose the cake he wanted, carefully pried the too-wide top off the pan and slipped a knife around the edges and down into the cup, wishing he'd thought to buy paper liners.

Steady. Steady. D'oh!

The cake crumbled in his hands. Okay. Okay. Five more chances.

He tried again. And again. And again. Damn it. Down to two. Maybe if they were cooler? He stuck the pan with the remaining two cupcakes into the freezer and ran to his room to get dressed, since his work clothes, which he'd selected that morning hoping he'd be seeing Angela later, were covered in flour and cocoa.

A pair of dark khakis, a little wrinkled, but they'd have to do, a shirt that matched pretty well...

Back in the kitchen, he grabbed the pan out of the freezer. Definitely cooler. Good.

He picked up the knife and started in with more confidence.

Bad idea. The second-to-last cupcake disintegrated also, though not as rapidly as the previous four. So he was on the right track, but down to his last option.

The pan went back into the freezer while Daniel shaved to spare Angela's chin—assuming she'd let him kiss her again—and good thing he did because his first glance in the mirror revealed a big streak of frosting on his forehead.

Back in the kitchen. Running out of time. Pan out of the freezer. Knife in hand, sweating, feeling like a brain surgeon, finessing the blade, coaxing the cake, urging it on, even talking to the damn thing in a high crooning voice he didn't think he'd ever used before.

"C'mon. C'mon out, little guy."

He was losing it.

And then finally...success. The last cake only cracked, didn't crumble. He transferred it to a saucer he had ready, holding his breath. Again, success.

Now, frosting. A big knife-full applied gently. Very, very gently.

Not gently enough. The cupcake shuddered and collapsed. Damn it.

It would have to be the thought that counted. He grabbed the saucer and, no longer needing to be careful of a gift for his beloved that looked like a sludge heap, sprinted out to the car. Five minutes to her house, he should make it in time.

Except halfway there, he remembered the most important part of this entire project was sitting in the pocket of the pants he'd taken off and he had to turn around and start the trip over.

Fifteen minutes later, he pulled up to the bakery. No parking spaces.

Damn it.

He double-parked. Got out to warn Angela he was there, see if she could get away. They could drive to Cal Anderson Park for his presentation of her bakery treat. If treat was the right word, which he wasn't that sure about.

It started to rain again.

Okay. So much for the park. And thanks, Seattle.

He ran inside Come to Your Senses and flung open the door to A Taste for All Pleasures. Scott was at the counter. Angela must be in the back.

"Hi, can you tell Angela that Daniel's here?"

Her helper gave him a speculative look. Had Daniel missed a spot of frosting? Powdered sugar in his hair?

"Angela's not here." Scott shook his head regretfully. "She left about an hour ago."

ARGH! IF DANIEL wasn't at his job, and he wasn't at home, where was he?

Angela sighed, letting her head bonk against the interior door to Daniel's building, and too bad about leaving a forehead mark on the glass. She shouldn't have sailed off like this. She should have called Daniel and arranged a place and time to meet, like a normal person would have. If for no other reason, to find out if he even wanted to see her again. She'd once again been swept away by the romance, swept away by the idea of showing up and surprising him.

Swept away by Daniel. But this time, she wasn't afraid of the sweeping part. Not anymore.

Okay, maybe a little. She was human after all.

She turned and stared through the exterior door at the rain coming down. Again. Maybe it would be best to—

Her cell rang and she dove into her purse to dig it out. It was Scott. Gulp. Trouble at the bakery?

"Hey, Angela. Daniel was here looking for you."

Looking for me. Angela practically took off and floated around the foyer. Daniel wouldn't be trying to find her if he were still angry.

"Is he still there? What did he say? How did he look? What did you tell him?"

"I told him you weren't here." He was laughing at her. She couldn't blame him. "I guess he took off."

He guessed. Damn. "Okay, not a problem. I'll find him, thanks, Scott."

She hung up and pressed the phone to her cheek, clutching the cupcake box between her elbow and waist. If she called Daniel where would she tell him to meet her? Back at the bakery? Here? Somewhere neutral? Maybe that would be best.

Legs appeared on the interior staircase, followed by a stocky torso in a casually fashionable suit. Daniel's roommate, whatever his name was, holding an enormous bouquet of flowers.

He opened the door, grinning at her, hair freshly combed back, smelling of aftershave. "Hey, little girl, lookin' for someone?"

"Hi. You're Daniel's roommate."

"Jake. We met across your counter."

"Jake, yes." She shook his hand. He looked a lot more cheerful than he had that day. Maybe undercover cookie-buying made him nervous. "Beautiful flowers."

"Yeah?" He looked at them proudly. "Got them from that cute girl with the store across from you."

"Bonnie? She's great."

"Seemed it." He tugged at a red rose to make it stand out more prominently. "Would you want to date a guy who bought them for you?"

She laughed. "Absolutely. Whoever she is, she'll flip over them. And you."

"I hope so, thanks." He blushed, grinning like a fool in love. Or was that redundant? "Daniel's not home. You want to go in?"

"I hoped he'd be here." She tried not to sound as frantic as she was. "I want to surprise him."

"Allow me." He whipped out his cell, punched in a number. "Yo, Daniel. Where are you? Uh-huh. Oh, she's not? You're— Okay, good. I'm out tonight with Valerie. Yes, *again*. Right. Okay."

He hung up the phone and beamed at Angela. "He's on his way."

Her heart started pounding. "Thanks, Jake. Okay if I wait upstairs?"

"You can do better than that." He unlocked the building door and pushed it open for her. "There's a key in the toe of one of the soccer shoes opposite our apartment. Let yourself in."

"I will, thank you." Perfect. *Perfect!* She'd be able to surprise Daniel in a big, big way. Preferably naked. "Oh, and have fun tonight."

As the door closed behind Angela, he nodded, tipped an imaginary hat and exited into the street.

Angela climbed the stairs to the second floor, remembering tenderly how she'd climbed these stairs with Daniel after her aborted evening at Noc Noc. Thinking how much hope and angst and effort people had to put into starting relationships. With any luck, after she got to talk to Daniel today, they could move forward without so much stress. Maybe without any.

Holding her cupcake box, she fumbled in the soccer shoe, trying not to think about sweaty male toes, grabbed the key and let herself into the apartment, then walked toward the kitchen to put the cupcake box where Daniel would—

Whoa.

The kitchen looked as if a baking bomb had gone off. A mixture of flour, or confectioner's sugar or both, and cocoa powder coated surfaces near the mixer, on the floor and even on the cabinets. On the table, saucers of chocolate cake, crushed in strange mounds, surrounded by mangled crumbs. A muffin pan with more cake clinging to it. Next to that, a small bowl, half-full of grainy, streaked chocolate frosting.

Jake's idea of a snack?

Baking burglars?

The front door opened. Angela jumped. She'd wanted to greet Daniel sitting calmly and stark naked on the couch but this could be Jake coming back for something, so it was just as well she was clothed.

"Jake?" Daniel's voice.

Angela suppressed nervous laughter, heart lifting as if it had been pumped full of helium and hope.

No, it wasn't going to be the romantic setting or situation she had in mind when imagining her apology and, she hoped, their reconciliation. But then their entire first date had consisted of settings and situations she hadn't imagined, either, and it had turned out to be nearly perfect. Maybe that was part of the good lessons she was learning, not to count too hard on things going exactly the way she expected. Maybe that's what Jack had been trying to tell her when he talked about the model for his new series.

"Angela." The pleasure in Daniel's voice and face dimmed when he took in the wreckage around them. "Uh. I was going to clean later."

"Exploding grocery bag?"

"I made cupcakes." He produced one very, very sad specimen on a plate, and put it on the kitchen table, clearly nervous. "Um. Actually, as it turned out, I only made one cupcake. Or something approaching the concept of cupcake. For you."

"Thank you." She put her single-serving box next to the plate, embarrassed that her gift turned out to be one-upmanship. Though it would be hard to do worse than the one he'd made. "I brought you one, too. I'm sure yours is much better, though."

They both stared at the brown mangled mess he'd made, and then they both started cracking up. Nervously, yes, but it was good to be laughing together again.

Really good.

"Angela." He took a few steps toward her, his blue eyes cautious. "I'm sorry I was—"

She held up her hand to stop his unnecessary apology, impatient to explain. "You have nothing to be sorry for, Daniel. I'm the one who was pigheaded and blind to what you and several other people were trying to tell me. But I hear now. I understand. I'd be really, really proud to have my cookies at Slatewood's Spring Fling and I'm very grateful to you for making that possible."

"You're…" He looked completely taken aback at her transformation. "Wait, really?"

She laughed. "Really, Daniel."

"Wow." He grinned, put his arms around her, nearly making her swoon with how wonderful his body felt against hers. Where it belonged. "Turns out I'm going to this party you're catering."

"Yeah?" She slid her arms around his neck, leaning back to beam into his dear, wonderful, handsome and highly sexy face. "Who with?"

"This incredibly hot woman I've fallen for. Pretty hard."

"Oh." The smile faded from her face as happy tears fought to replace it. "Is she worthy of you?"

He nodded somberly. "More than worthy. Super-worthy."

"I'm glad." She shifted her pelvis deliberately back and forth, feeling a deliciously firm and quick response from his…pants. "You're in good company, because I've fallen, too."

"Really." His tone stayed light, but his arms tightened around her. "Someone I know?"

"Better than anyone."

Their kiss was long, deep, and so full of passion that their bodies could only follow. In two minutes, Angela was naked, up on the kitchen table, legs spread wide, breathing hard as she watched her lover's beautiful condom-covered erection slowly disappearing inside her.

Oh, Daniel. He filled her body, he filled her heart, his thrusts took her up and up until she braced herself on the smooth wood.

This was how it was supposed to be.

Except for the chocolate cake crumbs smushing and slipping under her palms. And, ow, her tailbone jarring occasionally on the hard surface.

Could they never get a break?

"Angela." Daniel made an inarticulate sound of frustration. "I want to be able to kiss you. I want room to do…everything."

"Yes. Yes." She put her arms around his neck, wrapped her legs tight around his waist. He lifted her, carried her into the bedroom, tumbled her back on the bed, and then, yes, then he could make love to her slowly, in total comfort, kissing her mouth, her face, her shoulders, her breasts, as if every part of her was his to savor, to adore, to worship.

She so liked that about him.

For her part, her hands were never still, kneading and stroking the smooth firm muscle of his back, his shoulders, the enticing curve of his buttocks.

And when the desire grew to where it couldn't be contained anymore, she locked her feet around his calves and strained up against him, push and release, faster, harder, no longer afraid of losing control. They came together, eyes locked, breathlessly ecstatic both in body and heart.

Then slowly, slowly, they came down together, and the love and tenderness in Daniel's eyes, the warmth and sweetness of his kisses, and Angela's response to both were so powerful tears came.

"Sweetheart." He brushed them away, one side and then the other. "Can I cheer you up with a cupcake? Or I should say, *the* cupcake?"

She laughed, still sniffling. She'd rather lie here and enjoy the afterglow a little longer, but Daniel was obviously proud of his hideous cupcake, and she was touched that he'd gone through such outstanding difficulty making it for her. "I would love it."

He was gone two minutes, came back with both cupcakes on a tray, along with a couple of glasses of milk. "This isn't dinner. I'll take you out later. If you're free."

"I'm free." She traced the line of his shoulder, down to the fine long fingers handing her the plate. "Except I'm not, am I?"

"No. You belong to me now." He stroked hair off her face, a gesture she now recognized as his way of telling her he cared about her, wanted to protect her. "And vice versa."

"That makes me really, really happy." She knew she was looking about as goopy as she'd ever looked, and didn't care at all. She did belong to him. But also to herself.

"Angela." His voice got lower and a little shaky. "When I met you, I told you about a promise I made to Kate."

"Yes." She grasped his arm, something solid to hang onto in case she needed it. He was looking awfully serious.

"I'd like to make one to you, one that comes from a free heart, and from love that is very, very new, but which feels as old as I am."

Love. Angela held her breath.

"Could you try some cupcake now?"

Huh? Now?

"Ummm, sure." Angela looked down at the chocolate disaster on the saucer. She lifted the cupcake, which promptly disintegrated through her fingers.

And left something in her hand. Something hard. And round.

"What—" She caught her breath. White metal, two entwining loops, and a tiny diamond protecting the spot they joined.

A promise ring. "Oh, Daniel."

"I know this is soon. I know we have plenty of getting to know each other to do still, but this feels very right to me already. Will you wear it?" He smiled, blue eyes anxious, kissed her, then leaned his forehead against hers. "If you do, you won't have to eat that cupcake."

Angela laughed, tears cascading from her eyes, and

slipped the ring on her finger, where it settled as if it had always belonged there. "It's beautiful. I will wear it proudly."

He said her name reverently, pulled her onto his lap and kissed her over and over until they clung, breathless and smiling like fools. "I knew after our first kiss, Angela."

"The one in the rain that freaked us both out?"

"That one." Daniel grinned, brought her ringed hand to his mouth.

"I was gone after that, too." She stroked his hair, his firm jaw. Everything about this man was beautiful to her. "But I'm not freaking anymore."

"We're going to be really good together, Angela," he whispered. "All I ask is that you let me know what you're feeling and what you need."

"I will, if you'll do the same." She touched his cheek, wistful for the time she'd wasted trying to convince herself she hadn't fallen in love, when it was so obvious for so long that she had. After just one kiss. "There is another thing I will ask you to promise."

"Yes. Go ahead." He murmured the words into her hair.

"That you leave the baking to me…" She shifted off his lap, drew his face down, tasting his lips with her tongue, stroking his chest then letting her hand wander lower to signal she was ready for round two if he was. And oh, goodness. He was. "But that together, we spend a whole lot of time…*cooking*."

"Mmm." He got her drift immediately, lowered her to the mattress. "A wide variety of *hot* dishes?"

She pursed her lips. "Smoking hot."

"Fancy, sophisticated cooking? Or ordinary, everyday?"

She pretended to think this over. "We'll experiment. And then do only what we have a real talent for."

"Hmm." Daniel settled his hips between her legs, started a gentle rocking motion. "I don't think that narrows it down much."

"Well, then…" Angela spread wider for him, let him see the joy and mischief in her eyes. "We'll just have to keep doing it all."

* * * * *

PASSION

COMING NEXT MONTH
AVAILABLE APRIL 24, 2012

#681 NOT JUST FRIENDS
The Wrong Bed
Kate Hoffmann

#682 COMING UP FOR AIR
Uniformly Hot!
Karen Foley

#683 NORTHERN FIRES
Alaskan Heat
Jennifer LaBrecque

#684 HER MAN ADVANTAGE
Double Overtime
Joanne Rock

#685 SIZZLE IN THE CITY
Flirting with Justice
Wendy Etherington

#686 BRINGING HOME A BACHELOR
All the Groom's Men
Karen Kendall

Julia McKee and Adam Sutherland never got along in college, but somehow, several years after graduation, they got stuck sharing the same bed on a weekend getaway with mutual friends. Can this very wrong bed suddenly make everything right between them?

*Read on for a sneak peek from
NOT JUST FRIENDS by Kate Hoffmann.*

Available May 2012, only from Harlequin® Blaze™.

"DO YOU REMEMBER the day we met?" Julia asked.

Adam groaned. "Oh, God, don't remind me. It was not my finest moment. My mind and my mouth were temporarily disengaged. I'd hoped you'd find me charming, but somehow, I don't think that was the case." He took her hand and pressed a kiss to her wrist, staring up at her with a teasing glint in his eyes.

Julia's gaze fixed on the spot where his lips warmed her skin. "Does that usually work on women?" she asked. "A little kiss on the wrist? And then the puppy-dog eyes?"

His smile faded. "You think I'm just playing you?"

"I've considered it," Julia said. But now that she saw the hurt expression on his face, she realized she'd been wrong.

She drew a deep breath and smiled. "I'm starving. Are you hungry?" Julia hopped out of bed, then grabbed his hand and pulled him up. "I can make us something to eat."

They wandered out to the kitchen, her hand still clasped in his, and when they reached the refrigerator, she pulled the door open and peered inside.

Grabbing a carton of eggs, she turned to face him. His hands were braced on either side of her body, holding the door open. Julia felt a shiver skitter over her skin.

HBEXP0412

Slowly, Adam bent toward her, touching his lips to hers. Julia had been kissed by her fair share of men, but it had never felt like this. Maybe it was the refrigerator sending cold air across her back. Or maybe it was just all the years that had passed between them and all the chances they'd avoided because of one silly slight on the day they'd met.

He drew back, then ran his hand over her cheek and smiled. "I've wanted to do that for eight years," he said.

Julia swallowed hard. "Eight?"

He nodded. "Since the moment I met you, Jules."

Find out what happens in NOT JUST FRIENDS
by Kate Hoffmann.

Available May 2012, only from Harlequin® Blaze™.